To Grace and John,

without whose valuable help it
would have taken far longer
to have written this.

1

'My Love Affair with Paris'

Contents

The Boss

One of the most colourful persons I have met is Hameen; he was larger than life. Even in his sixties, he broke women's hearts, including his long-suffering wife's.

A Muslim, born in Iran nearly seventy years ago, Hameen is completely westernised after an English university education. Although he inherited property from his wealthy family in his native country, he chose to settle in London and establish an international research company.

Our daughter, Diane, after completing a two-year post-graduate course in business studies, was recruited by him as a junior trainee. To make our acquaintance, he invited us to lunch in a restaurant near Victoria Station. Charm personified, he made eyes at me; my better half considered him to be rather flamboyant.

However, it occurred to me that our daughter, after a sheltered upbringing, would benefit from his worldliness, his sense of humour. The ease with which he dealt with other people would guide her into the international business world.

Hameen was not a handsome man: he was of slight build, with lively, deep-brown eyes - mischievous when in female company - very smartly dressed in a dark grey striped business suit, a black and grey striped silk tie on his immaculate, white shirt. An epitome of the figure of a gentleman of means, he slaved away like a workaholic, driven by a deep-seated competitive urge.

Naomi, his wife, accompanied him to Diane's wedding reception in a well-known hotel outside London many years later. Her loud voice, uncontrolled laughter and outlandish antics after several glasses of wine seemed to the other guests completely out-of-place. Oblivious of the disapproving looks her husband shot at her, she fully believed that her behaviour suited the occasion.

Of Jewish descent, she had met Hameen at university. Their completely different backgrounds challenged him and attracted her. Young and enthusiastic, they genuinely believed they could change the world by building bridges between Jews and Arabs, forever in conflict in the Middle East.

As they matured they had to admit, like so many disillusioned, broadminded Arabian and Jewish intellectuals, it was not in their power to heal the wounds which Israelis and Palestinians had inflicted, and are still inflicting, on each other.

They decided to start a family. Naomi, totally engrossed in motherhood with her two baby girls, realized - when it was too late - that she had neglected her husband. In the meantime he had found consolation in the arms of a young woman and had rented a luxury flat for her near his office. His scandal-loving secretary - her hopes of seducing him foiled when he was at a loose end - 'spilled the beans'. At first, incredulous, his wife ignored the news of "the gossiping bitch." However, when he absented himself for whole weekends her suspicion was roused. In her husband's suit and coat pockets, emptied in his absence, she discovered the mistress's address in a little note book. As soon as the baby's nanny arrived, she drove to the apartment building and scrutinised the names printed on little cards near the bells by the entrance.

"Good god," she shrieked, "they call themselves Mr. And Mrs. Namdar, as if I did not exist."

An acrimonious divorce was the result. She was awarded custody,

Haseem being the guilty party. His alimony gave her and the children security; at regular intervals he was allowed access to them.

Hameen's roving eyes settled on Diane, his young employee; she was thoroughly absorbed in acquiring the essentials of the profession. Single-minded, the twenty-five-year old gained full mastery of writing reports. She explored every possible contact in the market place which would furnish her with the information required by the client.

To reward her dedication, he offered her a junior partnership in the firm, thus tying her more closely to him. She was euphoric when she returned home that evening.

"I smell a rat," was her father's reaction. "To put it bluntly," he quipped, "your boss is not only gratified by your budding business acumen - he is just after your body."

Both mother and daughter thought this was hilarious and burst out into peals of laughter. "Oh, so typical of men with a one-track mind," her mother sniggered.

As it turned out, her father's observation proved to be correct. A few days afterwards Diane came home with, "Hameen feels I am too old to live with my parents. He wants to set me up in a *bijou* flat near the office."

"You see," her parent crowed, "his wicked intentions were so obvious to me. Right, that's IT: you'll hand in your notice tomorrow. There are other jobs for you out there."

"No. I stay put. I have already made it clear to him I do not want a sugar-daddy. Either he treats me as a valued junior partner or I quit."

Mother and father looked at their daughter with parental pride. Diane had become a responsible business woman, completely sure of herself and she remained. Hameen acknowledged that he had made a big mistake and humbly apologized for his unsolicited suggestion.

Over three decades have passed; Diane still works for him on a freelance basis, occasionally visiting clients with him, if she can absent herself from commitments as wife and mother.

The Boss has aged well. He had changed little when I saw him a couple of years ago, nor does he look like a man approaching his seventieth birthday. His libido must be exceptional for Sheila, a blue-eyed blonde, his last, young live-in girlfriend, was thirty-five years his junior. She nursed high hopes that they will marry and start a family. Clinging to him like a leech, although he had tried several times to shake her off, she pestered him with her demands.

Hysterically suspicious of Diane's relationship with HER lover, she was plagued by lurid scenarios: Hameen had made sly overtures to the virginal trainee when he had first hired her and, no doubt, she fantasized, "they were still at it, surreptitiously, in some hotel or even a flat in my absence." She could not overcome her fear that he was cheating on her.

The few times she saw them together, she watched them like a hawk, analysing every one of his and her gestures and sifting every word for hidden meanings.

"Today, my dear," he informed Sheila one morning, "Diane is going with me to a start-up meeting with a new client in Manchester. I have to leave early and I will get home late. So don't worry."

She heard alarm bells ringing: her worst fears had been confirmed.

"They're still at it," she murmured under her breath, but turning towards him with an enchanting smile, "Hameen may I come with you, please. I have not been out of London for ages."

He agreed in the belief that his 'side-kick' - she loved to shop and he was forever paying her bills - would be content to buy a whole new wardrobe. She always pointed out to him, "I want to be attractive, so you can show me off to your friends."

She did not get out of the car near the shopping centre, as expected; she stayed put, insisting that such a meeting would be a most valuable experience for her in her future career as a business consultant.

"You will be bored stiff listening to the technical element of the research project," he protested.

Diane was aghast; yet she kept quiet until after the meeting.

No other alternative open to him and against his better judgment, Hameen took her along; he introduced her,

"Sheila is my new intern. I apologize that I have not forewarned you of her presence."

Instead of keeping *stumm*, the silly girl regurgitated his project outlines to the men facing them. She firmly believed she was contributing to the discussion. No one listened to her; eventually she shut up.

Diane, fuming, expressed in no uncertain terms afterwards, "If she comes with us again, you can count me out, Hameen."

One late afternoon Sheila arrived at the office. Concealed in the shadow of the door, she heard snippets of conversation. "How is ..." - she could not make out the name - "love-life progressing? Surely by now..." - again she could not hear the rest, but did not want to get closer.

In fact THE BOSS was enquiring whether Diane's son had lost his heart to one of his fellow-students.

"You are a funny guy, Hameen, with a one-track mind. The answer is NO. He enjoys a wonderful social life, but his main aim is to leave in three years with a good degree."

Hameen was not deterred. "Next time I see him I will give him the benefit of my vast experience."

"Don't bother. When he is ready he will know exactly what to do", and they left it at that.

Sheila could not contain her rage, firmly believing that the conversation had been about her and her lover's long-term salacious involvement with her hated rival.

Bursting into the room, she screamed at the top of her voice, "Now I know the truth about you two. There is no more need for you to invent coded messages when I am present." Raising her voice to the highest octave, she blasted loud enough to be heard on the floors below, "my parents were dead right.

They didn't want me to get mixed up with a bloody Muslim foreigner. Every one of your ilk double-crosses, cheats and murderers, like ISIS."

That was the final act in their volatile affair. When she returned to the flat, she found her bags outside the door; a locksmith was busy changing the lock.

A week later, still very much game to explore new relationships to enhance his love-life, Hameen was introduced to a very attractive forty-five-year old widow with grown-up children who had left home. Once again his charisma worked wonders. She moved in with him. But being worldly-wise and prudent, she kept her own house just in case it would all go 'pear-shaped' and she would have to admit that she had made a mistake.

The ideal Husband

In 1939, shortly before the outbreak of WWII, they arrived in this country on a Kinder-Transport from provincial towns in Germany, leaving their parents behind. Benjamin was a thirteen-year-old, Esther was three years his junior.

In the train they had been sitting in corner seats by the window opposite each other. The black-haired, sensitive boy could not take his deep-blue eyes off the blond girl. Tears were streaming down her pale face; her frail body shook. The accompanying adult next to her made vain efforts to calm her, looking round for help.

"Können Sie mir bitte sagen, wie das Mädchen heisst," the boy said. (Can you please tell me the girl's name.)

"Esther."

"Danke. Darf ich sie ansprechen? Vielleicht kann es mir gelingen, sie zu trösten." (Thanks. May I address her? Perhaps I can console her.)

"Ja. Bitte." (Yes. Please.)

Benjamin bent his face towards her; the space between them was very narrow. He tried to take her hands in his. Shaking violently, she withdrew them.

"Esther, ich musste auch meine lieben Eltern verlassen. Ich weiss genau, was du fühlst. Aber für uns jüdische Kinder gibt es keine Zukunft in Deutschland im Dritten Reich. Unsere Eltern haben uns nach England geschickt, damit wir ein normales Leben beginnen können." (Esther, I too, had to leave my dear parents. But for us Jewish children there is no future in Germany in the Third Reich. Our parents sent us to England so that we can begin a normal life.)

Full of concern, he spoke so softly, looking straight into her tear-stained face; she became calmer and listened to him.

On arrival at Victoria Station they were met by families who were prepared to foster the young refugee girls; the boys were met by a young man from a Jewish hostel. He took charge of them.

Both children were of school age. Esther's new home was near the hostel; they were both enrolled in the same educational establishment. It was not surprising that at first they were completely disorientated in the new environment, by their lack of understanding the foreign language and different customs mystified them. Yet, luck was on their side. Ester's foster parents were members of the local liberal synagogue, so were the hostel's matron and warden, a married couple. They had always acknowledged each other in the street or after attending *Shabbat* services. Therefore, when Bejamin spotted Esher among the congregants, he rushed towards her as soon as he could.

Esther, too, was thrilled to see a familiar face. He realized that she had started to settle down in the middle-aged couple's home. With great pride he addressed her in English to show her his newly acquired language skills; lessons had begun the day after their arrival. Esther's generous foster parents had engaged a young student to teach their ward.

At first both were puzzled by the grammatical rules - so different from those of their native tongue. Due to their able teachers and hearing English spoken throughout the day the youngsters made swift progress. The boys had not been allowed to utter a word of German after two weeks within the warden's and the matron's earshot. Benjamin and Esther noticed that their German teachers' accents in the Jewish school had been poles apart from the spoken words they were learning.

They were admitted to the synagogue's religion school. Their Bar Mitzwah and Bat Mitzwah were celebrated in Esther's home and in the synagogue's youth club. Wherever and whenever they met they were seeking each other's company. By the time they had reached their high teens, they had fallen in love.

Esther, an avid reader since her childhood, became a secretary in a publishing firm. Shortly after her appointment, she asked her superior if she would be permitted to read some of the manuscripts piled up in the editor's office. Mr. James removed a few from the 'slush bucket'; he had considered them unworthy of his attention.

"Let me know how you rate these," he said, when he handed them to her.

Not many days later Esther told him, "You should have a look at Mr. Franklin's work. He is completely unknown, but I rather think his novel might appeal to the young intelligentsia, should the book be published."

He followed her suggestion and, indeed, the young secretary's opinion was proven to be right: four editions were printed and subsequently translated into other languages. As a result, she was promoted with an increased salary, commensurate with her new duties..

In the meantime Benjamin had also started earning money as a junior in an accountancy firm. There were no financial obstacles to prevent the young couple from getting married. The reception took place in the synagogue's large hall. No expense was spared by Esther's foster parents whose generous dowry was the down-payment for a semi-detached property, as well as furniture chosen by the newly-married.

"How much I would have liked my parents to witness this happy day," said Ben when they started their short honeymoon. "They would have been relieved that I am going to share my life with you, with someone with the same background. It was love at first sight, though I was too young then to realize it."

"You are my ideal husband," she whispered into his ear before they went to sleep a few nights after they had returned. "I like to go shopping with you, admire your culinary expertise and everything else which makes our life together more wonderful than I could ever have imagined."

Esther remained at home after the twins were born. Yet, because her husband was such a help in the house, she managed to edit books when the children were asleep. As soon as they were at university she returned to her full-time job.

The couple's 'cup was full'. Every so often they would repeat to each other, how proud their parents would have been of the twins.

Eventually their offspring flew from the nest. Both tried their luck in America where their qualifications were valued much higher than in England; prospects of faster promotion beckoned.

Esther and Ben had approved of their moving abroad, though they missed their presence, especially on Holy Days. When their sons were in their late twenties news arrived that they were marrying American girls. It was then that their parents fully realized they had lost them to the 'New World'. However, as soon as they were met at the airport both of them put on brave faces. Before the joint-wedding they were introduced to the brides, two sisters, and their family. The girls' mother and father had also been born in Germany, but had been able to join relations in New York shortly before the war. Although they were Americanized both parents had much in common.

Their sons had rented a luxury suite in the hotel were the reception was held. Esther and Ben had enjoyed all the festivities after the wedding ceremony; once they were back at home they knew the needs of their sons' families would always overshadow theirs; their grandchildren would grow up as complete strangers.

By that time Esther and Ben had reached their mid-fifties. All the excitement took its toll on Esther's health. She began to suffer from vertigo, especially first thing in the morning. Usually, she went down to get everything ready for breakfast about seven o'clock, had a shower and dressed before shaking Ben out of his deep sleep.

One day his wife's pitiful cry woke him up; she had fallen down the stairs. He jumped out of bed to help her. Desolate blue eyes looked up at him. With a monumental effort he hid his fear, feverishly thinking of an immediate plan of action. He phoned their G.P., Dr. Greenberg, a close friend, who hurried to them straight away putting a warm coat over his pyjamas.

"There is not much I can do for Esther, except ring the hospital for admission. I will explain what has happened and - above all - we must not move her."

A few minutes later, the patient was carefully put on a stretcher by the ambulance crew and driven with Ben on board who had hurriedly dressed himself, to the nearest hospital. The accident seemed to have paralysed her from the waist down. She was unable to stand on her feet. Her upper body was not affected: she could use her arms and hands freely.

After being discharged from hospital she was treated in a private orthopaedic clinic. Daily physical as well as psychological therapeutic treatment helped her to cope with being handicapped. Four weeks later it was considered safe for the invalid to return home where grips on walls, a stair-lift and other aids had been installed A bed which could be raised at both ends had been delivered and a carer had been employed.

Esther adjusted well to the circumstances in which she found herself, hoping that sooner or later she might be able to walk again. Ben was completely stressed out, fully convinced that his wife would always be wheelchair-bound and that their idyllic life together had ended. To him the future seemed like a dark tunnel without a glimmer of light. It hardened his character; he became negative. The gentle 'ideal husband' metamorphosed into a strong-willed man.

Their sons arrived for a brief stay. They had been given short compassionate leave by their employers and could hardly believe the changes which had taken place in their father's demeanour and behaviour. Where was the 'ideal husband', as their mother used to call him? At their wits end, they consulted Dr. Greenberg who had been their doctor ever since they were born.

"What has happened to our father? Everyone called him the 'ideal husband' and he was a wonderful father to both of us. We never heard a harsh word from him. When we had been silly, he used to reprimand us, that is true, but he always took great pains to explain to us what is right and what is wrong. Decisions about the household he left to our mother who very capably managed to be there for all of us. There was always harmony in our home, a good example to us now that we are parents ourselves."

"This is the only way Ben is able to deal with the complete reversal of their plans after retirement. They had dreamed up a scenario of visits to you, travels to the Continent and spending enjoyable leisure time with their large circle of friends. Now all their hopes are shattered, so it seems to him. But your mother is a fighter; she will not give in so easily," he concluded.

Very slowly, almost imperceptibly, Esther made some progress with the assistance of a twice daily carer, supplied by an agency. Rekha was enormously strong; she lifted her on to a stool in the bath, washed her, gave her a shower and dried her, dressed her, supported her while she sank into the wheelchair, eased her into the stair-lift and a second wheelchair at the bottom of the stairs. She pushed her into the dining-room for breakfast. Before leaving. she tidied everything upstairs, washed-up, cleaned the kitchen and assisted the patient to sit in the sitting room, facing the television with the remote control and library books on a small table beside her easy-chair.

Mature women, with grown-up sons, client and carer found much common ground, though the latter's background was Indian.

"I envy you," Esther commented when she was ready to move to the stair lift. "Your sons are in London, still living at home. Ours could not get away fast enough to seek their fortune in America. I wonder if I will ever be able to fly to New York again."

"Of course you will. One of my clients - she can hardly use her arms and hands and her speech is slurred - travels all over the world to where members of her family have migrated. The stewardesses on planes are specially trained to make handicapped passengers as comfortable as possible."

"Rekha is always so positive, so unlike Ben." Esther said to herself later and, as time went by, carer and client became great friends, sharing past experiences. Rekha found new ways to strengthen the invalid's legs with daily massages and exercises she had been taught by the physiotherapist who came twice a week.

His wife's relationship with her carer had a devastating effect on Ben. "Rekha has hijacked my wife's affection and made it her own alone," he tormented himself when he spied on them. "My wife has no idea what her behaviour does to me."

After a year he had worked himself into such a state of excitement and rage, driven by sheer jealousy because "the intruder is destroying what is left of our marriage", that he terminated the contract with the care agency. As he sounded so irate, even threatening, the agent wisely ignored the fact that he had to give at least a month's notice, not just a day. In the event she refrained from handing the matter to her lawyer, fearing bad publicity would harm her business.

The following morning Esther, completely ignorant of Ben's hasty decision, expected Rekha's arrival, as usual.

"We had better phone the agency to find out why Rekha has not come," she shouted from the bedroom. At that moment Ben was preparing their breakfast in the kitchen.

"She won't be coming anymore, my dear," he informed her as he entered the room. "You were getting too pally with her, telling her intimate things which should be kept in the family. The care arrangement has been cancelled."

"Who will help me now? A different carer? I will have to start all over again to explain what I am expecting of her. Rekha was just right for me - now it will take ages for a new person to take over from her successfully."

"There won't be a new person," he retorted abruptly, raising his voice. "I am taking over. Who is more qualified than I am after all these years?"

She was livid.

"And you did not bother to consult me? It is my welfare that is at stake - and we are not short of cash. Humour me and satisfy my curiosity: why did you sack her?"

"It's your fault. She had become more important to you than I have ever been."

In a moment of shrewd insight, his wife taunted him. "Admit, you envied us, the manner we communicated, like good friends."

Ben left the room in fury; he returned when he had shaken off his anger.

"Let's get started."

Trying to smile, using all the strength he could muster, he heaved his wife into the wheelchair. He had watched Rekha: the manner in which she supported the invalid under her arms and lifted her on to the stool in the bath. Esther clasped the grip on the wall. He washed, showered and dried her clumsily, lacking the carer's expertise. Dressing her in the bedroom after he had wheeled her back was as great an ordeal for his wife. She was relieved that after shifting her into the stair-lift and the wheelchair at the bottom, he had managed to settle her at the dining-table where breakfast had been laid. Utterly exhausted, he served continental breakfast, consumed his own in haste, cleared the table and washed up, while mentally preparing the shopping list.

Ben refused to admit that he had taken on too much; he relied on his iron will to overcome his tiredness. He gave up his hobby, resigning from the local bowling club he had belonged to since his retirement about ten years previously. He missed the company of his fellow-members and the matches for which he would be selected. He resented he was tied to his wife day and night, although he had inflicted that on himself.

Esther watched in silence and dismay how the physical and mental strain took its toll. He showered her with abuse when she uttered what was in her mind.

"You cannot carry on like that," she begged him when she felt he was ready to collapse. "If you have financial worries, our children would gladly step in and pay for Rekha's services; they have offered it so often."

"I am not going to be beholden to our sons. No way! What we do is none of their business," he shouted, his face crimson with rage.

She shrugged her shoulders. The matter was dropped.

For over a year Ben acted as his wife's full-time carer. He grew weaker; it became more and more difficult for him to cope. In vain Esther implored him not to let his pride and obstinacy destroy his health. Again her pleas were ignored. The inevitable happened. He had a heart attack; this occurred at the best possible moment in the morning after breakfast; Esther had wheeled herself into the sitting room and was reading the newspaper. At least she was safe.

Ben had just entered the room to check on her and he collapsed with a loud thud on the carpet beside her. Immediately she pressed the red button on the alarm she wore on her wrist which connected her to the local helpline. She had not lost her presence of mind. Contact was made; she explained what had happened

An ambulance came shortly afterwards. A paramedic examined him.

"I am afraid it has been fatal, madam. Your husband is dead. At least he did not suffer."

The body was taken away; his female colleague stayed with the bereaved and administered some medication so that she would overcome the shock. She contacted the couple's children and rang Rekha, Esther's former carer, to find out if she was free. And, in spite of this dark moment in her life, there was a chink of light: Rekha had just returned from India after two months' holiday and was able to be with her former client every day, even over night, if required.

"No. This is not necessary. You go home once you have settled me in bed. I am much stronger than Ben would ever believe. Everything I may need is near the bed. Don't worry, I will be alright," she assured her. "Just be back tomorrow at seven, like before; I am so happy you are taking care of me again."

The sons arrived with their wives; the grandchildren had stayed behind with a far-distant cousin. They arranged the cremation which took place as soon as possible; the death certificate had been issued when the body had been released by the coroner. Esther insisted to be present, but was not at all moved by the officiating rabbi's words. According to her, as she mentioned to her family, "he was just mouthing the details you gave him about Ben's life."

After the funeral her family gathered round the dining-table. She informed them that she would sell the house, a detached property in an up-market residential area. She would instruct the son of one of Ben's friends, an estate agent, who could be trusted to look after her interests.

Everyone looked at her aghast.

"Without discussing it with us first! And where will you live with your mobility problems?"

"In a nursing home where my friend Jane lives. We had lost touch but her daughter supplied the address."

"So you had it all planned while Dad was still alive," one of her sons uttered.

"Yes. I knew what was going to happen, the way your father was carrying on. I had to be prepared" she stated, like a matter of fact.

Everyone struggled to keep up with her future plans. Her sons remembered how decisive she had always been when they were children. It was she who ruled the roost; their father - as they had whispered to each other - was besotted by her. He never interfered which they had considered a sign of weakness.

Esther continued. "It was a challenge to live with Ben during the last couple of years, to endure his violent outbursts because he did not want to admit - even to himself - that he was incapable of replacing the carer. But in spite of these violent outbursts while trying his best to do everything for me, he had made sure that, apart from this property, the interests on his investments would always keep me financially secure."

"Mummy, didn't he leave anything to us?" one of them murmured.

"No, dear," she answered calmly. "All his estate was left to me. But don't despair you two," she sniggered, "when I am dead and gone you will inherit whatever is left, shared in equal parts. I signed the new will a couple of days after the cremation while you were entertaining the other mourners. But you can take anything you fancy: paintings, silk ties, electric kitchen equipment - take your pick."

Disgusted by the unwelcome news their mother had just dished out to them, they did not take a single thing.

Esther felt at home in the spacious room in the nursing home where a therapist was treating her regularly. She had brought some of her favourite possessions: family photographs, memorabilia collected for decades and her favourite Impressionist painting, 'The Pink Dancers' by Degas, which used to hang over the mantelpiece in her lounge. She shared memories with Jane, enjoyed the fortnightly entertainments arranged by the management and outings to shopping centres with Rekha and mobile residents, supervised by one of the nursing staff.

Often her thoughts wandered back to the past: the happy years she had spent with Ben, their sons' childhood and teenage years. With hindsight she found it extremely difficult to comprehend why it had all ended in misunderstanding and strife. But after a short while she pushed the darker memories out of her mind and concentrated on the fact that for the first time in years she felt relaxed, looking forward to what the next day had in store for her.

Not long after her admission to the nursing home the residents' doctor told her that the therapist had great hopes of improving her condition. The good news delighted her.

"He is a highly qualified man and teaches students at the British School of Osteopathy. He has intimated that he would be very keen for your progress to be filmed to illustrate his lectures. No doubt, he will talk to you about it when he sees you tomorrow."

As soon as he had arrived Allen Baker mapped out the treatment he had envisaged for her. "We will get you moving, though it will be a slow process, my estimate is three to four years; it may entail some spinal surgery - a MRI scan will give us a clearer idea. My intention is to get you out of the wheelchair on to a Zimmer frame after holding on to parallel bars sliding your legs, followed by wearing callipers and eventually walking with crutches. If you agree to being filmed, my fees will naturally be reduced," he said, looking at her eagerly.

"Of course, I do agree. When do we start?"

"Now!"

The scan revealed no spinal damage. Vertebras had hardly shifted; it was the complete lack of exercise and movement, imposed by her dictatorial husband, which had stiffened her leg muscles to such an extent that they refused to function. When this was pointed out to her, she was greatly relieved. On the other hand she regretted that, once recovered from the shock of falling, she had not stood up to her husband. Her usual positive spirit had failed her.

"All the years I have wasted - no, both of us have wasted. We could have enjoyed the rest of our lives together; he would not have had to change so drastically," she said to herself.

With utter determination she made slow progress which was recorded daily. The callipers were uncomfortable, as she was only used to soft materials round her legs. But she persevered; within a relatively short space of time she managed to push herself forward with the frame.

The seasons passed; she did not lose heart. Her family visited her just once. They were surprised how cheerful she was, but she could not refrain from injecting an ironic remark when one of her sons asked her about her improving mobility, "You are only trying to find out when you can inherit my estate." They let it pass, pretending not to have heard it.

When watching the offspring and grandchildren of the other residents, aware of the affection they lavished on their grandmother or grandfather, she blamed herself. "Did I show my twins too little love?"

The truth was that the younger generation did not know how to handle their handicapped mother. For them it was out of sight, out of mind.

Spring had arrived early. Ether longed to go out. "I want to see the world, be among younger people. I want to renew my wardrobe, powder and make-up my face like the 'normal' woman I used to be," she murmured under her breath, "not like the others sitting around, their half-closed eyes staring into the distance."

Allen, always waiting for the patient to be ready to go that little bit further, suggested, "You are ready to be driven to a shopping centre with your Zimmer frame. Remember you have been 'out of circulation', so avoid crowds."

Esther booked a larger hire car, recommended to her. With her trusted carer she got to the shopping centre early in the morning straight after breakfast. The outing was a great success. She bought wide trousers, loose blouses and knitted garments, as well as a lighter coat. She felt elated and could not thank her patient and compassionate carer enough.

The daily exercises were still continued. Her body responded; the muscles and ligaments which had been tightened during her inactive years gradually extended. Esther began to make plans for the future. She consulted Allen.

"Am I ready to move into a sheltered flat, or am I too ambitious?

"Go ahead, provided your carer spends a couple of hours with you twice a day to make sure you are safe when you get up and go to bed, prepares a meal you can heat in a microwave and sandwiches for the evening. I would advise that you have your dinner at lunch time and go to bed early; above all do not tire yourself out. Of course, your treatment will continue for the time being."

Rekha and Esther viewed sheltered flats, some empty and some furnished in the neighbourhood familiar to her, in close proximity to local supermarkets. Three weeks later she found exactly what she had wanted: three rooms, a well-equipped kitchen, separate toilet and bathroom. She bought it on a ninety-nine years lease. Most of her furniture was brought out of storage with her priceless possessions; arrangements were made for the rest to be sold.

With her carer pushing a walker, she managed to do her shopping; driven in hire cars, she visited shopping centres, went to local restaurants with friends. One very special friend made it possible for her to go to the theatre once or twice a month.

"I have to exercise my dormant brain cells; some intellectual activity or input would surely enhance my existence and keep me occupied," she reasoned once she was completely installed in her new surroundings. She talked to elderly neighbours one of whom advised her to join the local University of the Third Age.

"At the monthly meetings speakers talk about a variety of subjects; you can join interest groups: high- or low-brow; groups go to theatres and art galleries."

Soon afterwards she attended one of the meetings, studied the various announcements on the notice-board and decided to pay her first annual subscription. After further reflection she chose two interest groups.

"There is no need for you to book hire cars to drive you here and back," the secretary informed her. "I will pick you and get you home again."

After a decade of trials, she thoroughly enjoyed life again: above all, she was in command of her own destiny. Less and less she ruminated about the unhappy time she spent with Ben, his intractability and how different their Third Age together could have been.

The Interpreter

Klara, a sixteen-year-old from Vienna with a catching sense of humour and the eldest in the refugee hostel for Jewish girls from Central Europe, had befriended Hannah. Two years her junior and still very naive, she regarded her as a fountain of wisdom. Grown-up in less sheltered surroundings, Klara knew how to fend for herself. After her seventeenth birthday she moved out; she was able to support herself.

Hannah was distraught. "You will forget all about me; find new friends; get married," she moaned.

Sunday mornings the girls used to gather in the spacious day-room to attend English lessons. The teacher's parents originated from Germany. They spoke their native language at home: their daughter grew up bi-lingual.

A blackboard on an easel, propped up in a corner of the room, was placed in front of Miss Joseph's pupils who sat on the carpet facing her. She had written on the black surface, "I want to be...when I am an adult" and a list of occupations and professions. She asked her pupils, "What do you want to be?"

One of them stood up, pirouetted, and called out, "I want to be a ballerina!"

Another announced, "I want to be a *Malerin*". "A painter," translated the teacher and smiled.

"And you, Hannah, what do you want to be?"

"A professor, like you: I always wanted to be a professor."

"I am not a professor, just a language teacher," Miss Joseph corrected her.

By that time Klara had become impatient; as the eldest her turn was the last. Her knowledge of English was relatively advanced.

Painstakingly she had read the books on the shelves and had tried to make sense of the rules in the grammar book, donated by the committee ladies responsible for the hostel. With pocket money saved for weeks she bought a second-hand dictionary.

"How do you say *Dolmetscher*? That is what I want to be," she spouted.

In the early forties of the last century all able-bodied young people were employed in some form of war-work, if they had not been called up. That also applied to Jewish refugees from Central and Eastern Europe who had been classified as 'Friendly Aliens', Category C, by a magistrate at the beginning of the war.

The shortage of munitions was acute. This country had been ill-prepared for modern war-fare, largely due to the appeasement policy by the Chamberlain Government. Factories which used to manufacture nonessential goods were turned into munitions factories. Shift-workers on production-lines were employed day and night.

Klara, a free spirit, did not like to be regimented in the Army. It suited her to put on an overall, hide her reddish hair under a scarf, both issued to the girls. At break, away from the infernal noise of the machines, she chatted with the others. Being gregarious, she soon made new friends among her English colleagues who were impressed that she made herself understood within a few weeks and liked her sense of humour.

Hannah missed her older friend on whose judgment she had always relied, believing that Klara had shut her out of her mind. Yet, one Sunday after two years, she appeared unexpectedly.

"Matron told me your new address. What a nice room you've got - and you keep it so clean! You must be the youngest in the boarding house. Are the women boarders mothering you?" she asked. "I guess they are all refugees, like us."

Klara, ready to impart her exciting news, was too impatient to wait for an answer.

"I am getting married to a German young man. As I am only twenty years old, I did need matron's permission. (In those days the Age of Consent was twenty-one.) She vetted him, a serious fellow, who is twenty-six, commenting that Hans will keep me in order. He also works in the factory. Since last year we have been going out together. Now he has proposed to me and I said 'yes' straight away. Yes, he will try his best to keep in on the straight and narrow." With that she burst out laughing.

After the wedding ceremony - Matron gave the bride away - the reception was held in the hostel's lounge. The girls who had learned to cook prepared the buffet: sandwiches filled with delicacies and a choice of home-made pastries.

It turned out to be a very festive day; for a short while the young refugees forgot about their past and their forebodings about a future without any parental guidance. When everything was cleared away, they played the records Klara's English friends had brought with them and danced.

Before the couple left, Klara promised Hannah faithfully she would not fail to keep in touch with her; "Hans will remind me to do so - and you look after yourself."

By the time Hannah was independent, living in a boarding house, she had found her own circle of friends: fellow-students of the University Extension Course in the Department of Education; she was still pursuing her hopes to become a teacher. So intent on keeping abreast with the course-work, she hardly ever thought of Klara. When least expected her former friend turned up. Matron had given her the address.

Hannah could not hide her joy. She carefully put her half-finished essay into a folder and embraced her friend.

"Long time - no see," she called out. "How are you and Hans? Preggers, yet?" The questions spilled out of her mouth like running water.

"I have sued for a divorce," was the laconic reply.

"Divorce? Why? You seemed so suited to each other. Has Hans been unfaithful? He did not strike me to be the type who would look at another woman."

Klara thought that was hilarious. When she had controlled her outburst of laughter, she explained, "Hans, sleeping with someone else? No, never. He is much too dull for that, poor soul. On grounds of incompatibility, but it will take ages until I am free," she complained.

"What do you mean? You both have the same background, shared the same experiences. So what went wrong?"

"I want to have a LIFE! I'm not like you sitting around the house, hunched up over books. Now that the war is over - and we can afford it - I want to go out, see the bright lights. So our marriage did not work out; we were so inexperienced at the time - he should not have been at twenty-six. Most men have at least broken two hearts," again peals of laughter. "He was still a virgin, would you credit it! Anyhow, we decided to separate, or rather to divorce. Perhaps both of us will find someone else."

"I bet you have already someone in mind, more to your liking," Hannah joked.

"It's no laughing matter. It's sad - and the answer is NO." To emphasize her statement she banged on the table. "I am going to reconstruct my life completely. An acquaintance told me that the Americans need interpreters -

German speakers, preferably former Jewish refugees, to visit the concentration camps; the brief is to resettle the surviving inmates. I have applied, passed a language and intelligent test. I am going to be an OFFICER in the US Army once all the formalities are completed. By the way, my name is spelt Clara, now. What? Why do you look at me like that?"

"Because your parents, like mine, perished in the Holocaust - you are not the right person to meet camp inmates."

Hannah's voice, usually soft, shouted in outrage. It had torn at her heart-strings when she had visited the Holocaust Exhibition in the Imperial Museum. With her compassionate husband she inspected the model of the camp with the lethal furnaces. She almost broke down there and then, especially at the sight of a mountain of shoes and personal belongings which had been retrieved from the unholy site.

The very last news Hannah received from Klara was shortly after her marriage to a former German Jewish refugee. By a sheer fluke of fortune she had remembered her new surname. It was Berliner. (Many Jews chose names of the towns to which they had moved once they had been permitted to leave the ghettos.)

For over seventy years Hannah had not corresponded with Klara, until by sheer chance she found a photo of her in US uniform and the unit in which she was serving. She was smiling, seemed relaxed in her brand-new outfit. Wondering what had become of her friend, Hannah downloaded information about the liberation of Dachau and the names of the personnel who had been drafted into the camp to offer help to survivors. Her patience was rewarded; she located her friend, a widow like herself, living in New York.

Without delay, she sent a letter with a brief summary of her own life in those decades, adding her e-mail address, as well as her telephone number, suggesting they could meet up virtually on SKYPE. By return of post a letter arrived from Klara.

"I have a computer," she wrote but my brain is not equipped to cope with all the various programmes. But when my daughter visits me we can talk to each other. I will ask Lisa to bring her lap-top."

There was the difference in time - eight hours - to contend with, as Hannah mentioned to Lisa, when she rang.

"It does not matter at all. Mother has to be up early. They serve breakfast in the nursing home from 8.30 a.m. to 9.30 a.m. and sometimes, as a special favour, until 10 a.m. So the virtual date with her is Sunday next."

Hannah was delighted. Over and over again she read the instructions how to download SKYPE given to her by her grandson. At the appointed hour Lisa, rang. She introduced herself; then her mother's face appeared on the desktop. Her hair was completely white, though she had aged so well, that Hannah could still discern vestiges of her former regular features.

There was so much they wanted to tell each other about their life since they had parted. Yet, strangely enough, they referred again to the days they had spent in the refugee hostel. Klara - Hannah she would always spell Klara with a 'K' - said very little about the time she spent with the US Forces; she hardly alluded to the victims in the camp. Some instinct forbade her friend even to broach the subject. It struck her forcefully that Klara just reminisced about the early forties, remembering incidents she herself had forgotten.

They talked over an hour; or rather Klara talked non-stop, until Hannah was too exhausted to continue. They agreed they would meet again soon on SKYPE, now that they had found each other again and that they would remain in contact for the rest of their lives.

To her utter dismay, she received a most disheartening e-mail from Lisa the following day.

"My mother, after speaking to you, was so shaken, even mentally disturbed, by raking up the past. I am asking you to refrain from writing to her. Now she is completely unsettled again; I can only hope that she will become calmer soon. Please respect my wishes."

Piecing together the facts Klara had mentioned about her present life, it dawned on Hannah that she must have had a mental break-down, due to her experiences while serving in the US Army. Talking to her must have conjured up demons of the past, including her parents' fate, both victims of the Holocaust. Her brain was so unhinged her daughter feared she might have a relapse into severe depression from which she might never recover.

Hannah concluded afterwards, "I was absolutely right when I had misgivings about Klara's decision to go to one of the extermination camps where her parents might have perished. It was inadmissible of the US Army to recruit vulnerable young people."

The Peacocks

My sitting room walls are decorated with paintings, photographs, as well as memorabilia picked up while on holiday or given as presents. Some would say those walls are cluttered. It is difficult to choose the most precious momentous reminder of the past of the past.

The assortment of memorabilia - some oblong, some round - displayed on the wall of the sitting room have either been gifts or acquired during many travels abroad. The most striking image was handed to me at my retirement party over thirty years ago by Siva's father. Two colourful peacocks, their tail-feathers reaching the top of the white circular background, are embroidered in the middle of beige silk.

"Hindus value peacock's feathers. It is a sacred bird in our mythology; we believe they bring us good luck," he explained. "I pray they will do the same for you and your family. This is a small token of thanks. You have done so much for my shy daughter and my wife and I are very grateful to you."

Siva had a slight speech defect, a minor handicap compared to the wheel-chair bound, yet mentally alert, teenagers in the school. Her slow thinking-process caused her to give hesitant answers, some of them not even relating to the question asked. The school's speech therapist had tried her best but the girl remained very shy, mono-syllabic, frightened to be ridiculed by her peers.

Roy, her father, short, broad-shouldered was quite a character. Always cheerful, he could be counted upon to take photographs on sports and prize-giving days.

"He seems to have plenty of time and money. What actually is his business? I mean how can he afford to be available during the working week?" my colleague corrected herself.

I did not enlighten her, though I knew he was a wheeler-dealer, importing goods bought cheaply In India - carpets among them - and selling them at inflated prices in his shops in London and other big towns.

"If there is any advice you think I can give you, please ring me," I told him, before he left the party with his daughter.

At frequent intervals I received 'news bulletins' about Siva's activities and his future plans for her.

"Siva has been taught Indian dances. She will never excel in them, but she has become more graceful. Now at eighteen it is high time to find her a suitable husband in India. After Independence many of the princes are impoverished because of the high taxes imposed on them. Some have even turned their palaces into hotels in order to maintain themselves in style. A suitable eldest son, a maharaja, has been found by my friend who arranges marriages. Money is no object as far as I am concerned. I know they have abolished all the titles, but aristocrats are still respected."

It was not up to me to protest. To take their daughter away from the environment into which she had been born seemed an abhorrent idea, especially as she only spoke English. It was a complete lack of understanding. The 'lure' of becoming the father-in-law to a prince over-ruled every other consideration, as that would enhance his standing in London's Indian community.

Siva's mother, Vayu, was powerless; her husband's words were final. She travelled with him and their daughter to a northern province in India. During the ten-hour-long flight she tried to prepare her daughter for what was to become of her.

"When you are married you will live in Dharma's house. All daughters-in-law become part of large Indian families, not like your Mum and Dad and you in our lovely London home. That is the custom. You will have to obey your mother-in-law's orders implicitly."

Vayu simplified the meaning. Siva had to fully understand what she was trying to explain to her; it was the most important advice she could give her. "You just have to obey and carry out every one of her orders, otherwise your life will be very difficult."

The young girls looked bewildered. Never before had her mother addressed her so seriously. She had been used to her home, always sheltered and the centre of her parents' affectionate attention.

"Why are you giving me away then, in a foreign country, Mummy? Don't you love me anymore?"

"It's not a foreign country," Vayu replied with tears in her eyes. "It is the country in which all of us belong. Daddy brought me here to England to make a better living, like our other Indian friends."

It was all beyond Siva's comprehension. She watched silently as her mother packed the new silk saris which would flatter her petite figure and the silver rings and sparkling armbands she had bought to impress the bridegroom and his family.

Soon after their arrival, once the dowry - an enormous sum - had been paid, her marriage to Neel was celebrated with great ceremony and pomp. The festivities were so lengthy that the young bride was almost unconscious when she was driven with her husband to her mother-in-law's princely estate. By the time the marriage had been consummated, she was too exhausted to even realize what had happened; her mother had not instructed her about the facts of life. It would have frightened innocent Siva to death.

Next morning, bleary-eyed and mystified, she felt the body-heat of Neel, her husband, next to her. When she discovered the she sheet under her was soiled with blood, she cried.

He jumped out of bed. In anger, he shouted, "You silly girl." His loud voice echoed through the adjacent rooms, alerting his mother; she threw the door open.

"You are backward," Dharma scolded the frightened young bride. "Didn't your mother teach you anything? I do think half the time you even don't understand what anyone says to you."

Months had passed by; Siva did not become pregnant. She submitted to the rough nightly coupling; it repulsed her; she sobbed silently after the ordeal. Finally, the doctor informed

Dharma that that her daughter-in-law was unable to bear children. Insults were heaped upon her by everyone, including the other sons' wives. Neel satisfied his strong sexual urges in the arms of a mistress. Thoroughly disenchanted, he yelled, "Roy, my father-in-law, has deceived us: he has tricked me into accepting inadequate goods."

Everyone in the household ridiculed her; treated her like dirt. The most menial tasks were assigned to her. As she failed to carry them out according to her mother-in-law's satisfaction, Roy was summoned.

"Take your incapable daughter back to England with you. We don't want her here," the matriarch spit out. "And we must be compensated for her failure to perform the duties expected of the wife of a prince. You should never have had the audacity to bring her, damaged goods, to us."

Having paid what Roy called 'an exorbitant ransom', father and daughter flew back to London. Siva's mother was appalled at the sight of her: the bloom on the once lovely face had been replaced by deep lines. Her bewildered eyes revealed she could make no sense of what was happening to her. Like in a trance, she moved slowly around the house, sometimes tripping over her own feet. A carer was employed to look after her during the day. When she kept falling out of bed and began to sleep-walk, her parents decided with a heavy heart it was necessary to find a place in a nursing home for mentally-disturbed patients. There she faded away before her twentieth birthday.

Afterwards, Vayu accused her husband daily. "You, with your ideas of grandeur, are responsible for Siva's mental decline and death. Now, because of you, I have lost the child I loved so much. I will never forgive you as long as I live."

The rumour of his daughter's return from India and her disgrace had spread like wild-fire within the Indian community. Roy became a laughing-stock; the business-connections he had envisaged, did not materialize. When the death of his daughter became known, they did rally round the bereaved couple who stayed in the same house, like strangers, until they passed away.

The peacocks did not bring them any luck.

The Singleton

Laura – *Hannelore*, the birth name on official papers - was reminded of her first Continental holiday after WWII when, as a singleton, she travelled to Switzerland. The trip had been organized by the Teachers Union. After attending a few branch meetings, she was so disenchanted by the futile discussions that she did not renew her membership.

At that time it was still frowned upon for women teachers to be married. Her headmaster stated categorically, "Married women's attention is only partly centred on pupils. If they are mothers it is worse; they juggle to keep their maternal commitments on hold." Therefore, the couples in her group were male teachers with their spouses.

Moira and Laura shared a small room in the Swiss guest house. They became very friendly, exchanging facts about their past and present circumstances. Moira and Gerald, a civil servant, considered themselves 'an item', ignoring this generally accepted custom, though they did not live together. She had just turned thirty; he was two years younger, extremely eager to 'tie the knot'. Opposites often attract each other: Gerald was sober and serious; she was vivacious, forever wanting more.

"I have made plans to go to Australia. He does not know yet. Most likely I will find a teaching job. If not, something else will turn up in one of the big cities. They like to employ girls from this country because they speak The King's English," she said to Laura one evening.

A month before she was due to leave she informed Gerald of her plans. He was devastated, pointing out, "Moira dear, the clock is ticking.

You are not getting any younger and both of us want a family."

Moira laughed. "I'm as fit as a fiddle. So don't worry. I will return more experienced and wiser once I have got the travel bug out of my system. I will be ready to settle down."

* * *

The teacher in charge, Mr. Smith, in his middle fifties, treated his younger colleagues and their wives as he did his pupils. He was a short, grey-haired man, not much to look at. But when he issued his 'instructions' he seemed to grow in stature. The tone of his voice implied, "I want to be obeyed."

Before the war he had taken his seventeen and eighteen-year old students to Interlaken and was familiar with the region. He spoke German fluently with a slight English accent which Laura, a native German, detected straight away.

He was extremely fit; every day he drained the energy of all the members of his group during long hikes up mountain sides. Afterwards he commanded, "Have an early night. We start at 8 in the morning; it might be a strenuous day for you."

* * *

Gerald slept in a room adjacent to Moira's and Laura's. In spite of Mr. Smith's vigilance they managed to satisfy their sexual urges in a secluded spot of the deserted garden on a bench late at night. Mr. Smith, ensuring that everyone was safely tucked up in bed, patrolled the hotel grounds and, sure enough, he discovered the couple as they held their illicit tryst. Lost for words, he made his presence felt, tutting loudly, expressing his displeasure.

"We could not help laughing when he was out of ear-shot; we fell off the narrow bench," Moira said to her room-mate next morning. "He is so prim and proper. He does not understand young people. Not the best recommendation for a teacher."

Laura nodded, but she felt her behaviour was unseemly.

"If any of the Swiss hotel staff had noticed you, what would they make of the way English teachers conduct themselves?"

"You have a point there," conceded Moira. "We let our side down."

* * *

In the fresh mountain air the holiday was invigorating. London was so far removed from the idyllic scenery, the good food and the pastries in the *Café Schuh*. No other teacher in the group spoke German. Laura was in great demand as an interpreter when they trooped into the Café. She was always invited to choose refreshments, paid by one of the teachers. Unlike the others, she had limited resources.

The last day came too soon. The very idea of returning to the daily grind in London was hard to accept. Gerald pleaded with his intended to abandon what he considered to be a whim. Moira stuck to her plan, ignoring his distress and, before she left Laura at the station in London, she promised, "I will write to you. Please, please, try to cheer Gerald up while I am away."

* * *

During the autumn - spring in Australia - Laura received enthusiastic letters from her friend. Moira had travelled around, sleeping in cheap hotels and finding temporary jobs when "I am broke", as she put it. Finally in Melbourne Mr. Levi, an entrepreneur who had fled with his family from Germany in 1939, employed her in his family's export business, silk scarves and ties, designed and manufactured in the firm.

"We still speak German among ourselves. Even my son Heinz is incapable of composing correct English letters. All correspondence will be dealt with by you alone", he explained during the interview.

Jubilantly she informed Laura, "I have landed on my feet: with a very good salary I have been able to rent a small furnished flat. You MUST come to see me."

Shortly after her departure and for the next few months Moira always asked for news about Gerald, repeatedly begging Laura to check up on him without fail. But gradually she hardly mentioned him in her letters, as if he were of little importance to her.

"Heinz has introduced me to his friends; most of them are offspring of former refugees from Central Europe, interesting men about my age. My social life has taken off with a swing!"

Three months later, this letter, so full of the *joie de vivre*, was followed by an invitation to her wedding to Heinz. "It is a civil ceremony. They are Liberal Jews. I don't need to convert. Please come to give me away. The family will pay the fare and hotel bill."

* * *

Laura, committed to her job, could not leave mid-term. She was at a loss how to break the news to Gerald. He had bought and furnished a semi-detached house for his beloved's eventual return.

"Nothing is too good for her. Only the best will do," he kept on saying, when Laura had accompanied him to the various shops. "I rely on your judgment: help me choose what you think will satisfy her excellent taste."

He was so immersed in "the happy future with my darling", that only occasionally he wondered, "Why doesn't she write; I do miss her so much. The small room on the first floor will be the nursery. She can pick out the cot and everything else which will be needed."

In early spring he moved into the house. No more letters had arrived; he sent her a telegram, fearing that she had had a serious accident.

Laura could not bear to prolong the suspense any longer. One week-end she decided to break the bad news to him. "Gerald, I cannot keep the truth from you; I do not know how to lessen the shock. Moira is remaining in Australia. She is married."

"When? To whom?"

"To an Australian of German-Jewish descent."

"What's her name now and her address?"

Never before had Laura seen such a dramatic change in a man's expression and demeanour. Like an invalid, he sank into the light-brown sofa and wept.

Instinctively she put her arm round his shoulder, sitting next to him, and tried to comfort him. As it grew darker it was obvious that he could not be left alone: Gerald might commit suicide. Quickly she drove to her bed-sit, collected her week-end bag, always ready packed, and returned to him. At first he would not open the door; she did not give up.

He had worshipped the ground Moira walked on. Did her bidding, shared in whatever she had chosen to do. She loved walking; whenever weather permitted they wandered through the Hertfordshire countryside, stationing his car at a convenient place. It had kept both of them very fit.

He had neglected his friends, most of them colleagues from the office.

Laura encouraged him to go with them to football matches as he had done previously. They all commiserated with him, only too keen to welcome him back into their fold.

Laura's influence gradually dispelled his dark moods. In gratitude he invited her to theatre performances, aware that she had always been 'a theatre-buff'.

"It's the only way I can thank you for sustaining me mentally after her betrayal. I have been to pantomimes as a child, musicals as a grown-up. But with your guidance I am beginning to appreciate modern and classical plays."

Afterwards they would discuss the merits of the actors and the plays and, while doing so, they got to understand each other more intimately.

* * *

Almost a year had gone by. Gerald became more relaxed. Although he had been deeply hurt, he began to believe that a happier future waited for him.

Laura's motherly concern for his welfare turned into love; in his presence she hid her feelings. It was Tim, his closest friend who detected her ever-increasing affection for him.

"A wonderful wife for you stands in the wings: look in the right direction. Has Laura not saved you from sinking deeper and deeper into misery? Has she not been at your side whenever you needed a shoulder to cry on? Could you exist without her?"

"No. Not anymore. I would be lost," he murmured and reflected how he depended on her. "No. I could not be without her," he acknowledged and then, "I do wonder if I am also in love with her."

"Well, you should do something about it. She is 'a catch'. Don't miss the boat!"

Tim's words fell on fertile ground.

Laura, completely unaware of Gerald's budding love for her, could not conceal her surprise when he addressed her with, "I don't know how to start, Laura. Over the last few weeks your solicitude has underpinned my will to look forward and lay the past to rest. I have been so moved by what you have done for me and, Laura dear, it has made me fall in love with you."

She was so touched by his imploring eyes, that she stretched her arms upwards, standing on her toes, and put them round his neck.

"I thought you would never ask!"

They were married in the local town hall's registry office. Their friends were sitting behind them. A cold buffet had been prepared by the bride beforehand. After every one had finally left, they washed up, tidied the house and, for the first time, sank into their marital bed together. It was sheer bliss; so was their honeymoon in Italy during the school holidays.

In the meanwhile authorities had started to employ women teachers. But as their baby girl was born a year later, Laura gave up her post when her maternity leave had expired. She did not accept a new part-time job until her daughter was of nursery age.

Admiring their healthy, rosy-cheeked new-born sleeping peacefully in the cot, Gerald said softly, "At last the nursery is occupied."

* * *

Moira still did not want children which greatly distressed her husband's family who had lost so many loved-ones in the Holocaust. They had been appalled that Heinz had married a *Schickse*, a derogatory term for a Christian wife, and not one of the many eligible daughters in their community. His mother had begged him, "At least ask her to convert to Judaism."

Her son had laughed. "Mother you are still living in the past."

"And what about your children? They will be brought up as Jews, won't they?"

Heinz grew impatient with her for the first time in his life, raising his voice, "Let it pass!"

Moira had been very frank with him when he proposed to her. "Heinz, I do not want any children, not yet."

He had not taken her seriously and laughed, nor had his elderly parents. They often broached the subject and, finally, her mother-in-law confronted her.

"I am not ready for motherhood," she answered impudently.

"When WILL you be ready? Both of you are in your late thirties. You are the only childless couple among our friends."

Moira felt pressurized; the glitz of her new life was wearing thin; and, what she had not anticipated, was becoming home-sick. The truth suddenly dawned on her, "I have little rapport with the German-Jewish community. Why on earth did I get married to THEM. The Jews here do not just marry their partners; they get married to ALL the family. I am suffocated mentally and spiritually. I must get home and, if Gerald will have me still after the shabby way I treated him, I am even prepared – against my better judgment – to have his child."

Heinz was shocked when she announced her decision out of the blue.

"You can divorce me on grounds of desertion. It was a big mistake to try to belong to a community so completely alien to me. I am to blame, I alone – not anyone else."

Behind his back his relations and friends said, "It serves him right for marrying-out, seduced by the fact that she is so different from all the Jewish girls with whom he has been in contact since childhood." Yet they were all supportive because he was broken-hearted.

* * *

At the airport in London Moira rang Gerald in his office, certain that he was still single.

"I am back, my darling, "she gushed."I am ready to become your dutiful wife - that is, as soon as the divorce has been granted. Can I come? Are you still at the same address?"

"Moira, how can I soften the blow? I married Laura; we have a lovely baby daughter. You did not expect me to wait for you forever? I am sorry."

He put down the receiver. Moira never contacted him again.

Moira remained single, chastened by her self-inflicted misery, but wiser as a result. She concentrated on her career, became a respected headmistress before her fiftieth birthday, full of compassion for students and parents who sought her advice.

She retired after the summer term when she was sixty years old, sold her flat and bought a little bungalow by the sea-side in Essex. There she became an active member of The Women's Institute, tended her garden and finally found contentment in her Third Age.

The Proselyte

In the late forties – I was a very young teacher - a colleague of mine in her twenties surprised me with a strange announcement, "I have in mind to become Jewish."

"You are not serious? Nowadays, young people 'want out'; religion does not feature in their non-spiritual life-style and YOU want to 'come in' " I joked. "Tell me a valid reason to substantiate that."

"Recently I have read about the Holocaust, the suffering of the Jews and their fortitude. It is inspiring; I want to learn from them; perhaps it even rubs off. I want to be accepted into their faith."

To be frank, I did not take her seriously, believing that the high-spirited art-teacher got carried away. She left soon afterwards. She had vanished off my radar until I heard via the grape-vine that she had indeed been married to a Jewish young man in one of London's synagogues. It amused me that her confession had not been idle talk.

* * *

Michael, baptised as a Christian, has been admitted into the Jewish faith in his early eighties after studying Hebrew, Jewish history, laws and rituals for two years under the guidance of a rabbi. There is no trace of any Jewish feature in his face. In The Third Reich, during the middle of the last century, he would have been classified as an Aryan. The lonely individual, who spent most of his middle-years travelling and teaching in Russia, became unsure about his identity after retirement and returned to London. It occurred to me, as he spoke, that he was 'in limbo' after an active, absorbing career; he needed a 'spiritual foothold' to fill the void.

When in the premises of the synagogue, he wears a scull-cap, like an Orthodox Jew. "I take it off outside," he explained, "there is too much anti-Semitism nowadays."

Michael had dug deep into his mother's and his father's ancestral histories and discovered that in the 17th century a Polish Jew, married to a Christian woman, had fled with her to this country to escape the wrath of her family.

"You cannot imagine my joy. It proved without doubt that Jewish blood is flowing through my veins," he said when he sat next to me at one of the lunches for senior congregants of the synagogue."I have always felt an affinity with 'The Wandering Jew' and now I know the reason why."

"What about your family? Siblings? Cousins?"

"We have never been close, my younger brother and I. I do not need to justify my decision to him, nor does he care."

* * *

Michael felt safe in his new spiritual home. As an adult he had never been a practising Christian, except when his parents had pressurised him to attend Sunday School as a boy. Proud that he now could read Hebrew, a regular congregant at Shabbat services and other Holy Days, he never married and remained a loner.

After serving the dessert, the cook always offers 'left-overs' to be taken home. He, without fail and with one of his rare smiles, produces a plastic box which she fills to the brim. This might be the only healthy meal he eats.

* * *

For a couple of months he did not turn up. Nobody could fathom why. When he did show up, he was a changed man: Michael's face was snow-white;

he had a stubble of white hair on his chin as if he had not bothered to shave for a few days. His long hands, steady before, shook relentlessly. He had lost weight; the sports jacket drooped over his rounded shoulders. He approached the table slowly, supported by a solid stick. His face radiated fear; he looked like a wreck.

His good manners were so embedded in his make-up that he enquired, "May I sit next to you again?"

The meal had been served. It was pitiful to see how the soup spilled over the spoon as he lifted it to his lips with his right hand. Holding on to the white dinner plate with his left hand he again used the right hand to scoop up the hot meal, always careful not to drop food on the white paper table cloth. It needed his full attention and, only when he had finished. did he turn to me.

"I have had a nasty fall; it was lucky that I was indoors. I tried to lift myself up, but the effort was such that I passed out. When I came round I managed to grip a piece of solid furniture, somehow crawled to the telephone in the hall and dialled 999. The ambulance crew arrived; I shouted through the letter box, "There is a key-box on the left side of the wall", and told them the secret code. After that I must have blacked-out once more. When I regained consciousness I was in a hospital bed. Various tests confirmed I had mild concussion, though no operation was necessary. All I needed was complete rest, followed by rehabilitation to regain movement in both legs."

They were unable to discharge him until a care package had been arranged. I, too, was faced with a similar problem after back surgery a few years ago. Having had the most unsatisfactory experience with my council's social service when my late husband needed care - always different carers, never at the appointed time when he was so tired that he dragged himself upstairs and I had to undress him - I opted to employ someone through a private agency; the cost is somewhat higher than we had paid to the council.

"They come twice a day," he said. "They get me up, watch I do not keel over in the shower and while I dress, make my breakfast, and leave a cold lunch for me. In the evening they put the ready-meal in the microwave and, after dinner, make sure I land safely in bed."

He stopped for a few minutes to get back his breath.

"I want to go into a nursing home. I can no longer live independently."

"What about your furniture, your books, your cassettes? In a small room there will be not enough space for all the treasures you have accumulated during years of travels."

He fixed his watering eyes on me. "I have done with my books and the music I used to appreciate. I cannot be bothered to listen to them or to read. Quite frankly, I even don't care what happens to them. The welfare people can dispose of them. All I want is to live in peace and be looked after by qualified staff."

There was no hint of regret in his voice, only resignation that his present mental and physical condition had deteriorated to such an extent.

* * *

To give up independence in old age, is the most disturbing problem in my light. I hang on to mine because it is the most precious gift bestowed on me, apart from the love of my family. Unlike Michael, I would grieve if I had to part from the collected works of Goethe, Schiller and other great German dramatists, all bound in leather spine which my late mother-in-law had shipped to this country before the Germans could confiscate them during The Third Reich, as Jews were not allowed to possess German literature.

To move away from my home and sell the furniture, pictures and other souvenirs, acquired by my late husband and me over forty years, would leave me in 'no man's land'. I remember the harrowing impact it had on my mother-in-law four decades ago. Due to her failing health she had to enter a nursing home. In the oblong room, lined with white paper and sparse furniture, only a few objects could be accommodated; some had been rejected by the matron. "My girls work to a tight schedule and are unable to keep everything dust-free." She pointed to all the various things we had to take back; they still have an 'after-life' with me; I would not want to part with any one of them.

Therefore I find it so sad that Michael wants 'to delete' everything which appertains to his former, healthy and confident self. His name is on a waiting-list of one of the

Jewish nursing homes. Once admitted, he may find the security for which he craves. With his 'Aryan features', Christian background and itinerant past, he will stand out among the widows and widowers, all of them Jews, descendents of former Eastern or Central European ancestors.

The Paraplegic

Jean, a replica of Alice, my German-Jewish mother-in-law who was a heavy-built, white-haired matriarch, looms large in my memory. She used to sit at the head of the table at monthly retired congregants lunches, dominating us and laying down the law. Like Alice, proprietress of a boarding-house, she was loud-voiced and outspoken. She did not suffer fools gladly or anyone who was as strong-minded as she was. With the latter she was always at odds, trying to score points. Preferring a peaceful existence, I never argued with her; she would have rendered me mentally 'limp'.

The resemblance with Alice is so striking that I wondered why, being brought up in different countries and with different backgrounds - Jean's ancestors were of Polish descent, immersed in a different culture - their mental make-up was identical.

On further reflection, the answer became obvious. Both had been in charge of others: Alice 'lording it' over German-Jewish old people in her detached house in Hampstead in the early years of WWII and Jean, fifty years later, over her extended family numbering seven in her terraced house in Wembley.

Having visited her once, I cannot imagine where everyone slept. Family photographs covered her through-lounge walls and were placed in rows on her side-board. (This seems to be the custom in many Jewish homes: I was overwhelmed in two other houses by the array of photographs of parents, children at all stages through their life, grandchildren, grand- and great-grandparents and other family members decorating the hall and furniture in the dining- and living-rooms.) Probably the householder wants to be in close communication with the nearest and dearest. Many of them had passed away, many of those alive had moved to America or Israel.

* * *

Jean had been a dancer until marriage and motherhood claimed her undivided attention. She never volunteered where or with whom she had been on stage. I did not want to be too inquisitive. Nor did she ever reveal where and when she fell, or for what other medical condition she was wheelchair-bound.

With tremendous effort, her lips pressed tightly together, she somehow managed to get out of the front passenger seat at our destination with the help of the driver. Somehow he managed to ease her into the wheelchair, taken out of the boot of his car. One of the receptionists who had spotted her waiting in the forecourt of the synagogue rushed out to wheel her into the dining hall, transferred her to her seat and propped up the folded wheelchair in a corner nearby. For some reason she shunned electric chairs. It would have enabled her to get to the local supermarkets unaided, though her carer, on one of her good days, was able to get her to the bus-stop and into the bus which took them to Harrow. These outings she regarded as special treats.

In her home she moved around holding on to a small trolley. Her feet were very dainty, but strong. I do not recollect noticing a stair-lift; she must have dragged herself upstairs at night.

* * *

"I was a housewife with two children. My husband, Fred, in his late forties became an invalid after an accident at work. My parents needed supervision; I could not bear the idea that they might be shut up in an old people's home. Soon afterwards my widowed mother-in-law also needed care. So I took her in as well. It only seemed fair and was a great relief to Fred."

Silently I counted the number of grown-ups plus two boys squeezed into her house. The three rooms upstairs must have accommodated her family while she and her husband slept on a bed downstairs.

Peace did not always reign in the house, the older generation being set in their ways. The boys were continually reminded not to make too much noise with their pop music or when they played football in the small garden.

"I could not even allow that they invited friends, anxious that it might cause friction between the old and the young."

She hinted that she was always plagued by money-worries, but kept it to herself. Her family would have felt guilty for not contributing more.

"The boys' clothes cost a fortune. It was wonderful to see them grow tall, but trousers became too short, jackets and shirts too tight. Teenagers are always hungry; the old folk needed special diets. Somehow I learnt to put nourishing food on the dining table with special treats for Sundays, birthdays and our Holy Days."

There was another question I did not dare to voice. Again she supplied the answer.

"Three generations living together present other problems as well. Choosing a television programme, queuing for the one bathroom and toilet, petty quarrelling by the old people among themselves and with their grandsons. They did not know how to kill the time, literally waiting for the meals to be served. Apart from everything else, I had to smooth things over."

She sighed.

My mother-in-law, at regular intervals, had to warn her old guests who indulged in heated arguments to while away their waking hours that they would be thrown out without ceremony.

"I have a long waiting-list, so you had better watch your words," she admonished them in a determined voice.

But Jean did not have that option. Being herself high-principled she expected everybody to be like her. If anyone was less so, she told them off in her shrill voice; nor did she care that people turned their heads, shooting disapproving looks in her direction. She was a target of criticism by all those who did not appreciate her merits. These included sincere gratitude for the help received by social workers who admired the way she comported herself, always smartly dressed, sitting upright in the wheelchair at the table.

The hire-car driver who used to drive the two of us to the lunches picked me up the other day to take me to hospital.

"A wonderful, courageous old lady she was. I will never forget her", he said.

Expatriates

Nowadays I depend on hire-cars when I go to hospital appointments or the monthly lunches in the synagogue. Once only was an Englishman among the drivers. The others were born in Pakistan, Afghanistan and neighbouring countries where it is next to impossible to make a living or secure a decent education for the children; or they fear persecution on religious or racial grounds.

Seventy years ago in 1947, after the Partition of the Indian sub-continent, I was too involved with my professional duties to be aware of what was happening on the other side of the globe. Now I have the opportunity to make up for this gap and it always interests me to hear their stories. The similarities are remarkable and remind me of my own past: the persecution of the Jews during the Third Reich in the last century. When the affinity between our fates has been established, they are ready to tell me why they left their native soil.

*   *   *

Prahkash's command of English is almost perfect. He used to teach the language in India before arriving here with his wife and two children.

"There is no future for them there. In our schools teachers struggle to cope with about sixty children in a class; it practically boils down to rote teaching. If a child is left behind, there is next to nothing we can do."

I wondered why such an intelligent man was unable to enter the teaching profession here.

"I need to take exams to gain the recognised qualifications. This is time-consuming and, of course, I have to earn money. So I have no choice either at present or the foreseeable future."

He was stoic, yet full of hope.

"Both sons are very bright. Eventually they will go to university and enter a profession. My wife and I are quite satisfied."

* * *

Another middle-aged man hailing from Bangladesh had left his country with his wife and three children. His parents were ousted from India after the Partition about seventy years ago. They chose to move to Bangladesh, a predominantly Muslim country, rather than remain in Pakistan. But somehow he never felt comfortable in the new environment. To their eldest son they confided their anguish at leaving behind friends they had known since childhood and many of their possessions.

"It was the politicians who decided to carve up India on religious grounds. They completely ignored that most of us lived in harmony with our Hindu neighbours. Even our children used to play together. We spoke Hindi; I really cannot remember that there were any conflicts. Why did it have to happen? Whole families uprooted, torn away out the society in which they had thrived."

His mood was sombre. To lighten it, I complimented him on his command of English. "So many Asian drivers are speaking English really well."

"It was our second language. My parents insisted that my siblings and I should be taught privately. They had little confidence in what the school had to offer. Then I went to university and became a lawyer. Most of my clients needed help with filling in application forms for admission to England. And when I had been married for a few years to a language teacher, it was she who convinced me that we should come here for the sake of our three sons. Of course we spoke to them in English from an early age."

He stationed his car at a lay-by and produced a photo from his wallet. "The two eldest in their gowns on graduation day, both married now with good jobs. Our youngest is still with us. He has not yet made up his mind what he wants to do. He is only in his mid-teens." Looking at me with a sheepish smile, "He wasn't planned, but we love him as much as the other two."

"Are you happy here?"

"At home, 'yes'. But too many white people seem to prefer a white driver at the steering wheel. It shows in their faces. We are not accepted as equals because of the colour of our skin. Indians, who have been successful, look down on us, like on an inferior caste."

* * *

Paul did not tell me his name, but I gathered that he is a devout Christian. The name of one of the apostles fits him. He is a black South African, very street-wise, taking short-cuts, but his pronunciation and command of the language is not up to the high standard of the other drivers.

I prefer to sit in the passenger seat in the front. People's stories are often more rewarding than fiction.

"You are not from here?" At first I was not quite sure what he meant. Then it dawned on me that he had detected my slight foreign accent; unlike the others he was inquisitive. Having nothing to hide, I told him that I arrived here in my mid-teens as a refugee. He let my answer sink in slowly.

"A refugee? Why?"

I lingered before saying, "Because of racial persecution". He understood straight away.

"My folk know 'persecution' under apartheid. Terrible, terrible, terrible! Nelson Mandela, our hero. They were in townships, in huts. The Whites made us live like slaves, like animals. My grandmother was raped; there are half-Whites in my family."

Surreptitiously, this large, bulky man dried a tear with his handkerchief.

"But you can live with the White as neighbours." I rephrased, "You can live next to the Whites."

"Apartheid finished?" He shook his big head from side to side.

"South Africa has a government of black people. So is it not alright now?"

"Alright? No, no, no. There is no Nelson Mandela. They are swindlers." To make sure I grasped his meaning, he took a twenty pound note out of his wallet while we were waiting for the traffic light to turn green, held it up in the air with a sarcastic laugh, crunched it and put it in the pocket of his jacket.

"You understand?" I did, his mime could not have been more graphic.

"Motor cars: I had a garage when we moved among the Whites and a nice house. Good business: I am a motor mechanic, know all makes of cars, put them to pieces and whole again." He nodded his head in confirmation, before addressing me, "You got a car?"

"I cannot drive and sold the car when my husband died."

"Sad." His tone could not have been more compassionate. Returning to his previous subject, "All swindlers: Blacks stealing from Blacks. I speak Afrikaans, a bit like German, like the Whites. They speak English; they did not teach us in school. I only know easy words and cannot have a garage. But I can drive; that's how I earn money."

We had arrived in my drive. Before I tottered up the ramp to the front door I asked him to wait; sometimes my arthritic hands do not function. The key did not turn in the lock. He had watched me and jumped out. Somehow the lock had dropped; he, too, struggled for a few minutes, but did not give up. I took my little address book out of the handbag to find the local locksmith's phone number I had written down in case of emergency.

"It's open," he shouted with a smile and saw me safely inside.

"You spent much extra-time with me; you could have earned another fare." I took three pound coins out of my pocket, ready to give them to him.

"No. No tip. No money. We are here to help. God bless you, lady."

He took my hands in his and repeated, "God bless you lady."

The Shed

The shed at the back of my neighbour's garden has a story of its own. John constructed it himself in a hurry, eager to let his house. The residents in the well-kept bungalows near him grumbled incessantly. "This monstrosity devalues our properties."

The first lodgers were four nurses from the local hospital, three of them usually on night-shift. When they returned they made such a row that the one working during the day decided to sleep in the shed on a camp bed they had acquired.

However, they did not remain long. Everyone had complained about them, including us. John gave them notice, "And do you know," he told us, "they stole all the bedding, but left a camp bed in the shed."

* * *

After he had thoroughly aired and cleaned the house a mother and her middle-aged, pompous, over-weight son arrived. He fancied himself because he had attracted a few young females, lured by his melodious songs to the accompaniment of a guitar.

"Is the old girl completely deaf? The music does not seem to interfere with her sleep," my late husband wondered.

Every so often one of 'the chicks' would stay behind to be 'entertained' by him on the camp bed in the shed. Mother and son moved on a few years later.

* * *

Polish builders arrived next. Working from dawn to dusk in order to send money home to their families, we only met them after a couple of weeks when they introduced themselves. They were as quiet as mice, exhausted after a day's labour. With Mariusz, the first 'boss' of the team, I am still in touch after thirty years. Tomasz, his second-in-command, took over from him. His craftsmanship and that of his fellow-Poles was such that we, too, employed them for putting up a new fence and other jobs. His colleagues did not speak English and went home after a few weeks. The shed was used to store all their tools.

"It is so sad," Tomasz admitted, after we had exchanged Christmas presents, "that after fifteen years I only see my family at Christmas, Easter and a few days in the summer. My children grow up without their father; the little one thought I was a stranger." He sighed.

"Yes, fifteen years!" We looked at each other incredulously.

"But your wife came once before the last one was born. There is this nice garden and you had built a sand-pit and bought a rubber swimming pool. Why did they not come more often?"

"She does not like it here, cannot understand the language. Elaine, misses me as much as I do her, but here she feels isolated while I am at work. I know you tried to communicate with her while she was out in the garden; she was happy about that. I have really tried to convince her that the children would benefit from hearing English; my eldest has started to learn English in school. But she did not want to come a second time."

* * *

A year later Tomasz went home and John decided to down-size; George and I had done so in our mid-fifties.

"I will be seventy soon; my wife is in her late sixties. Our daughters have carved out their own lives, away from us. Our house is much too big for the two of us. We have decided to sell it and move next door to you."

Of course, I was delighted: two quiet people I had known for four decades. And, now, they have taken me 'under their wing', driving me to hospital appointments, going shopping with me and more. Their support is invaluable to me.

John with Tomasz who, much leaner now, has returned again to earn some money here is renovating the property as well as working for other people. During his stay he is sleeping in the loft which is a great comfort to me.

"I finally must clear the shed. I have kept all the girls' toys for sentimental reasons, It's a bit silly," he called out over the fence and then, as he opened it, he discovered that a vagrant had taken possession, his belongings stuffed into black, plastic bags strewn over the now ramshackle camp bed.

"The place is full of foul smells, unpleasant body odour; empty beer cans litter the floor. It's dreadful."

The following evening John lay in wait for the intruder, hiding in the dark. He did not stop him from entering the shed. In the morning he saw the dishevelled, unwashed man about fifty leave.

"I didn't think he would get that far, limping as he does and lurching from side to side," he thought.

Sure enough, John saw him sitting on one of the benches down the road.

"You have made your quarters in my shed. That won't do. Collect your possessions and move on."

The vagrant stared at him bleary eyed, failing to grasp what was said to him.

John, a true Christian, tried to save the alcoholic's soul.

"Here is twenty pounds, enough money to go to a shelter; have a bath, wash your hair and pay for a bed for a few nights until you have sorted yourself out."

The man grabbed the note with his filthy hands and toddled away on his unsteady legs. Yet, the very same afternoon, he was sprawling on the same bench, a plastic bag and empty beer cans at his side on the wet pavement.

"No one can help you, if you don't help yourself," warned John.

He thoroughly cleaned and disinfected the shed, partly rebuilt it with a strong wooden door and locked it with three bolts. He secured the end of the drive the same way. When he had done so, he rang the bell to give me a progress report.

"George called your shed an eyesore every time he looked out of the bedroom window."

"Why on earth didn't he tell me? I certainly would have done something about it."

And why didn't George confront him?

Germany's Post-War Generation

Thirty years ago, during spring half-term, my late husband and I visited the *Deutsche Bibliothek* in Frankfurt-am-Main. The librarian, Frau Mechthild Hahner, had written to all native Frankfurters of Jewish descent hoping to obtain personal correspondence and other relevant information for an exhibition. The German government of the day felt it was vital to remind the public at large of the persecution which lead to the Holocaust.

Frau Hahner was delighted that we had taken the trouble to come and meet her.

"It is sad that many Jewish people are still traumatised about what has happened to them and their families; they refuse to step on German soil, even to speak about it to their children. And that is exactly what has motivated us to mount the exhibition as a warning how a democracy -

though The Weimar Republic of the
inter-war years was a very young one
- can degenerate into a dictatorship."

* * *

Harald Roth, a history teacher in
Baden-Württenberg in his early
forties, considered it his mission to
enlighten the younger generation
about the atrocities committed by
their grand- and great-grandparents.
He described to them how every town
and village was *judenrein* (free of
Jews); they had been deported and
gassed in concentration camps. He
mentioned how many of their
neighbours and their former friends
had turned a blind eye, due to fear of
retribution by the authorities. As a
result, committed members of the
party, believing all anti-Semitic
propaganda to be Gospel-truth,
persecuted in gangs Jewish law-
abiding citizens.

Harald, too, visited the *Deutsche Bibliothek* to gather material for an anthology which could be used in schools. Examining the collection - all of it sent in by famous German writers and poets - bar myself and one other person - he spotted my contribution. I felt truly honoured when his letter arrived, asking me to write the story of my life in German. He added he would edit out or correct any mistakes in the chapters which were most relevant to the theme of his book.

* * *

After the publication of the anthology, '*Es tat mir weh, nicht mehr dazu zugehören - Kindheit und Jugend im Exil*', we met him for the first time at the *Frankfurter Buchmesse* in October 1989.

George and I recognised the tall man with short, blond curly hair, who strode purposefully through the crowded hall. I had enclosed a recent photo of myself in one of my many letters to him. We attracted his attention. Smiling, he approached us; we shook hands.

"Why don't you write a detailed autobiography which I will be happy to edit. My colleagues and I are starved of witness-testimony; your experiences pre- and post-war in France are also of great interest, as is your report about the Jewish immigrants you met in South America. So little is known! After the war - even many years later, due to the shortage of teachers - staff who had been members of the Nazi *Lehrverband* (Teachers Union) were re-employed."

Two years later, in October 1991 my autobiography, '*Frankfurt-meine erste Heimat*', was published and displayed at the *Buchmesse*. Being the author, I was invited with my family in the hospitality tent, rubbing shoulders with the great and famous.

It was an unforgettable experience which I am reliving as I am recording it.

A book launch in one of the local bookshops and talks in many schools and other educational institutions were well received; many copies were sold.

The English version, 'No longer Strangers', was published four years later. I still have the list of schools, retirement associations, social clubs, church mothers' meetings, and others - more than a hundred venues - in which I told my story. The high-points were eight talks at the Imperial Museum to A-level and university students, brought to London by coach from all over England.

The second edition was published in 2015 and is now available on Amazon as a paperback and on Amazon Kindle, as an e-book. Harald lit the spark which ignited my brain-cells. Three collections of short stories have been published since 2015; the fourth is 'on the production-line'.

* * *

The fate which befell victims and survivors gave my friend Harald sleepless nights. He had discovered that close to his home the Germans had marched 601 prisoners from *Stutthof* concentration camp near Danzig to the labour camp *Hailfingen/Tailfingen*.

"Who is willing to join me in creating a memorial and a museum at the very site where the slave labourers worked?" he asked his colleagues.

They were committed as he was. The museum, a mini-version of the Holocaust Exhibition in London, opened its doors in 2010 to receive visitors. Weekends lectures were given by Harald and his friends. A dwindling number of survivors speak to the visitors and guide them through the museum.

Now my friend is less active at the site; he has been replaced by a younger generation.

Those of us who were children in the Thirties of the last century owe a great gratitude to Harald. With the passing of decades, and the hatred of 'the other' in every corner of the world, the Holocaust would have been completely forgotten without memorial sites, reminders of human iniquity.

Snapshots

1 My Love-Affair with Paris

My love-affair with Paris began when I first learnt French as an eleven-year-old in the grammar-school. I had grown up in Frankfurt-on-Main, still a provincial town in 1933. Not one of the international commercial centres it has become after WWII, ugly tall buildings dwarf the precious historical monuments.

Our teacher, an enthusiastic Francophile, had shown us photos and illustrations of all the important Parisian landmarks. I was eager to see them one day myself. But I reasoned I might have to be older to really appreciate the French capital which had been described to us so vividly. However, the opportunity came already in 1938 for the wrong reason: the ever escalating anti-Semitism in the Third Reich.

My distant relations - *Tante* Wally and *Onkel* Jas - had moved their *atelier de mode*s to the French capital shortly after Hitler became Chancellor of Germany. They welcomed me in their home; I studied at the *Alliance Française* while I stayed with them.

After the war, a fully-fledged language teacher, I attended a course at the *Sorbonne*; with my pupils, later with my family, I returned many, many times. I wanted them to admire, like I did, what the French capital had to offer. Whether this resonated as much with them, I can only guess.

* * *

Our daughter, Denise, was probably in her fifteenth year when we climbed up to *La Place de Tetre* where artists, sitting on stools in front of easels, are plying for trade. One of them beckoned to us.

"*Mademoiselle, est très belle.*"

She blushed, trying to lead us away. But we were so excited that the painter had noticed her good looks; we lingered.

"Daddy took so many photographs of me. They are everywhere in the house. Why do you want to waste precious French francs?"

For once, we over-ruled her. Reluctantly '*mademoiselle*' gently got on to the stool.

"*Comment vous appelez-vous, Mademoiselle?*"

"Denise," she replied coldly.

"*J'aime ça - un prénom français.*"

He fixed a new canvass on the easel and took out his charcoals. After studying the contours of her face and expression intently, he drew a head and shoulders portrait of what appeared to us a much older version of Denise's features.

"*Voilà, ç'est fini!*" A satisfied smile spread over his face.

The portrait hangs in my sitting-room. Over forty years later, I am still pondering whether he had captured the 'real' Denise. Yet, he may have perceived an inner reflection of the sitter which we, the parents, were unable to detect.

2 Bled

In the mid-seventies of the last century we ventured for the first time into a Communist country. In all fairness, the main attraction was the considerably low cost compared with holidays in the West. The scenery, we were told, was magnificent.

Bled in Slovenia, part of the former Yugoslavia, situated by the lake, came up to our expectations. But we had not bargained for the fact - nor had the travel agent mentioned it – that we, from the West, were separated from Eastern tourists. We were 'hemmed in' in a small dining area;

our influence might have inflamed them with a desire for democracy.

Our taste-buds were used to *haute cuisine* when dining out and on holidays. The food was bland, though efficiently and politely served by immaculately attired waiter who spoke next to no English. We were certain that had been planned by the authorities: Yugoslavians might be subverted by visitors' opinions.

When we booked the holiday, nobody had warned us that most walks were off limit to us. May be the travel-agent was not even aware of this. The sharp eyes of the local tourist guides watched us relentlessly, even when we walked together in a group. But just once, my intrepid daughter and I 'escaped' while our minder had a heated argument with someone else. She was off guard, as far as we were concerned; we slipped out from 'under the net', promising my anxious husband that we would act like

Eastern tourists, unfamiliar with the language.

"You certainly do not look like those from the East. You better keep '*stumm*' ", he mumbled. "I promise to invent some plausible excuse should the 'leader' of our party notice your absence."

We absconded like naughty school boys. Our destination was a hill, not far from the lake. The air was like nectar; we were exuberant. I can still vividly recall the magnificence of that landscape.

The inevitable happened; we had lost our way. It was not a circular route, as we had expected and ended up in a village with a few houses. Although both of us were trilingual, the local 'lingo' was utterly incomprehensible to us.

"That's what happens when you are out of bounds," I joked. "It takes me back to my student days when I took risks climbing up mountains."

My daughter, made of the same metal as me, was exhilarated by the adventure which we were certain would end well none the less. Sure enough, an old 'biddy', in a long grey dress under an overall, was just shuffling out of her cottage in wide slippers to 'gape' at the strangers.

"We'll ask her. Don't worry," I assured my offspring. "I'll make myself understood, like in a charade game."

"*Madame*," was the only suitable word I could think of.

It registered; her face lit up. Perhaps '*Madame*' promoted her to a higher rank than 'woman'. The name of the hotel in Bled she had heard of and the word '*autobus*' brought forth a smile. Success: she had made sense of my gestures and words.

Punching the air with her arthritic left forefinger in the direction ahead of us, she signalled that we should follow her.At some distance stood the bus stop.

She was intelligent. Waving her stretched out fingers twice, she indicated we had to wait about twenty minutes.

I shook her hands and tried to thank her in all the languages I had at my command, adding '*Madame*' every time. She beamed at us and remained until the bus arrived and we were safely inside.

No doubt, in the evening she entertained her family and other villagers that she, the heroine, had saved foreign 'damsels in distress'.

* * *

Back in the hotel my husband's concern was increasing by the minute. Should he involve the tour leader? Perhaps it was necessary to send out a search party as lunch-time was approaching. The hotel management did not cater for late-comers.

This is the second time that we had caused him unnecessary grief. In Italy we had inspected the vineyards up a hill, also off the beaten track.

"Do you want to give me a heart attack, away from home? Here we do not even speak the language," he admonished the two of us. "And to penetrate into forbidden hinterland! What on earth..."

I cut him short. "We are back now, starving, ready for lunch."

"Promise me, never, ever to give me such a fright, otherwise I will not go on holiday with you both again."

I did give him my promise and kept it.

3 Mayerhofen

Once more, in my mid-twenties, I joined a teachers' group to travel to the Austrian Alps. A middle-aged childless couple, noticing that I usually walked on my own, befriended me. They were very knowledgeable; I learnt much in their company.

One evening the leader of the party suggested we should watch a troupe dancing the *Ländler* (a three-step waltz) and the *Schuhplattler* during which the dancers, all men in *Lederhosen*, clap hands, thighs and the soles of their feet, on a tribune which had been erected in the main square. After their performance couples were on the dance floor; none of us had joined in.

"Meez," a young sturdy man, perhaps a couple of years younger than me, in brown *Lederhosen* addressed me, pointing to the platform.

"Go on, have fun," my friends urged me on.

I gave him my hand and told him in German that I was not a good dancer.

"*Sie sprechen deutsch!*" (You speak German!) He brimmed with enthusiasm.

"Ich bin Sprachlehrerin in einer Schule in London." (I am a language teacher in a school in London.)

For a little while we danced in silence. He took great care not to step on my clumsy feet.

"You know," he whispered in German, "Hitler did many wrong things, but I fully agreed with his racial laws. The Jews in Vienna exploited the working class. He was right to put a stop to it."

For me the fun was over. When the musicians took a break I excused myself, dispirited that anti-Semitism was still rife in Austria. My companions, too, were disenchanted about the reminder of the past and took me straight back to the hotel.

4 Verona

One of the main reasons which drew us to Verona was 'Juliet's Balcony'.

There the teenage girl first caught sight of Romeo who had fallen in love with the daughter of his family's arch enemies.

In a photograph taken by my late husband, our daughter stands at a right angle from the Capulet's house - not underneath - in deference to the tragedy which unfolded in Shakespeare's play. The romantic story had not been his brainchild; he had based it on an Italian tale.

I saw two versions of 'Romeo and Juliet' many years apart. In the first the stage designer had recreated the balcony in Verona; the actors wore period costumes. One could imagine that similar tragedies had destroyed lives in a society where the slightest slur on a family's member's honour would unleash such rancour, leading to the death of two young innocent lovers.

On the stage of the second performance at the National the

setting was minimalistic. A knee-high, light-grey wall separated the couple in modern dress. The lines were beautifully spoken; to me it sounded false.

Many times recently I have been amazed by the changes which have taken place in theatre productions. Some, where the scenery had cluttered the stage with hardly any room for the cast to move about, have been cleared of unnecessary props. To the older generation, an almost bare stage is disappointing, though much more accessible to younger people. If it does encourage them to listen to the Bard's word, it should be welcomed.

The Artist

These reminiscences were triggered by photos posted on Facebook by the artist's daughter. They follow my late friend's life-cycle. The last one, which moved me, portrays Evelyn and her husband, Roy, walking away into the distance, their backs turned away from the viewer.

* * *

Climbing to the top of the stairs in my house, my eyes feast on the 'yellow daffodils swaying in the breeze'. The bright colours are enhanced by the light shining through the window on the right-hand side of the wall. It takes me back to my student days in the Lakes. The Liverpool college had been evacuated for the duration of the war. Evelyn and I wandered or cycled along the paths and over the hills.

Evelyn married a Welshman. The landscape of North Wales inspired her. With her easel and paints she used to amble not far from home: all of nature's handiwork around her. Many of her paintings were birthday presents to me. They vividly remind me of the many visits we paid her, usually in autumn, during our sixty-year-long friendship. With a picnic-hamper Roy drove us to a secluded spot. We sat on tree-trunks, the food and drinks spread out in front of us on a table cloth.

Two of her paintings on either side of one of her glorious water-colours transport me back to the carefree student days, enveloped as we were in the joy of togetherness.

One of her paintings, just outside the sitting-room, has fascinated me since the day she gave it to me and still does so now. It is in the style of some of Turner's works: an illusion of what she is seeing, similar to his

'Speed and Steam' (1843). The German poet and dramatist Goethe compared some of his paintings to 'The Morning of the Deluge', Moses writing the book of Genesis.

* * *

Evelyn did exhibit her canvasses in local galleries. Tourists were eager to buy them. She never agreed to sell these master-pieces. Instead they are decorating her friends' and her own house, inherited by her son and daughter. Recently I have been informed that the property has been sold. I wonder if her offspring have decided to put their mother's work on the market?

The Journalist

Isabella: I associate her with Isabella of Castile who, with her husband Ferdinand of Aragon, expelled the Jews from their homeland over 500 years ago. But Isabella, the journalist, is made of different mettle, with single-minded determination to act on the decisions in order to achieve her end.

The journalist, also born in the Iberian Peninsula, is a charming young girl in her twentieth year, concentrating all her energy towards her future career. Hers is a single-parent family. Isabella's father found a much younger 'model' and, in spite of being a devout Catholic, her mother Sofia, sued for divorce. It was granted to her. He married his mistress. They have a baby girl whom his daughter adores, nursing great hopes that they will be friends one day. Him, she rejects for abandoning his first wife.

Spain is one of the poorest countries in the European Union. There is no future for the young, unless their family have connections with influential people in high positions or their wealth opens doors for them. Therefore, Sofia took 'a leap in the dark': she decided to leave her birth-place behind, a small town, and all that was familiar to her. With the money she had saved, she came with her daughter to this country seven years ago. The UK still being part of the EU, no visas were required.

* * *

Having planned how to proceed, Sofia rented a small room in a run-down area in Paddington. For me, it is not difficult to form a picture of the place: a cupboard for a few clothes, a couple of chairs by a table and a medium-sized bed. As a seventeen-year-old, I was in similar dire-straights, earning a minimum wage. I cooked my one-course meal on a gas-ring near the fire-place. No Health and Safety did any checks then in lodging houses. Sofia's mother used a small electric appliance with two heating plates.

An ardent suitor, at least five years my senior far too possessive for my liking, offered to marry me. A qualified engineer, he was living in his own flat.

"The matron of the hostel who was in charge of you after your arrival has promised to give you away. All has been arranged; don't worry about the Age of Consent." And he finished, "I love you; I will do so for the rest of my life."

Since my childhood I had resolved to become a teacher. No one was going to stop me in my tracks. One evening, he was pestering me again, proposing on his knees. I showed him to the door. With hindsight, it was a cruel act; I should have softened the blow.

Through the refugee grape-vine I learned that he had resumed his relationship with the thirty-year-old whom he had left. In her arms, he was comforted; he married her.

* * *

Mother and daughter installed themselves in their new, cramped home. Then they wandered through the neighbourhood.

"That is a pawnshop, Isabella. I am going to pawn the jewellery and my wedding ring. It has no meaning for me anymore."

"How will you be able to negotiate with the man inside?"

Sofia smiled. "Do you think I am the only foreigner who enters his shop? We need a roof over our heads and money to buy food, like them."

After leaving the pawnshop they went to the local primary school. The headmistress was well-disposed towards them. As luck would have it, she spoke Spanish, enough for holding conversation. She listened to Sofia with sympathy.

"Isabella will only be with us for a year. If she works hard, she will learn English in the three terms."

She shook Sofia's hand. "I will make sure your daughter will be happy with us."

Isabella did work hard; the teachers were pleased with her progress. Being gregarious, she made many friends which further improved her language skills. By the end of the summer term a year later, her accent was perfect; occasionally she made grammatical mistakes.

Her mother had not been idle. The need to feed her child and herself drove her to the local labour exchange near the pawnshop.

"Any work will do, as long as I can earn our keep," she had said to Isabella.

"But, Mummy, you can type and do accounts, like you did in Daddy's shop. You even sold clothes to the customers and made notes of alterations required."

"Rubbish," replied Sofia. "All this has to be on hold. One day I will do again what I did before and earn good money."

* * *

Isabella studied single-mindedly in the technical college where she was enrolled after passing the GCSE. Naturally she had high marks in Spanish and was top of the year in French. Once she had completed her homework, she read voraciously books borrowed from the school and local libraries.

"You will have to come to some decision which particular course might appeal to you. Your teachers tell me that you are well-informed about what goes on in the world. Not every teenager reads newspapers. I respect that. Has it ever occurred to you to study journalism. Think it over; discuss it with your mother. It is a two-year course, not on offer here, but in a college nearby. With your good results and a letter from me you will be admitted and start early September."

* * *

In the meantime Sofia had been working as a cleaner. Evenings she went to classes to learn English; with her daughter's help she was almost fluent within two years, but she never lost her foreign accent. Spending her money wisely, she bought school uniforms, attractive tops and jeans for Isabella. She made do with what she had brought with her.

"You are a good-looking lady," Isabella encouraged her. "Your Spanish features will attract the 'right' man for you to marry."

"Don't be ridiculous. Not after my failed marriage to your father!" They never mentioned the subject again.

One day Sofia surprised Isabella on her return from college.

"Next week I am starting work in one of the West End stores, in the fashion department. The money is good with commissions on my sales. Soon we will move out."

Two years later, with the help of colleagues, she was able to put down a deposit for a small semi-detached house not too far away from the college and public transport. By the time Isabella contacted me, Sofia had been promoted to head-saleswoman with an increased salary.

* * *

Some months ago, a former neighbour rang me.

"Next door lives a Spanish student. Can she interview you? She studies journalism and thinks your past is very interesting."

Of course, I said 'yes' immediately. During my student days I had received so much help. Why not continue such a worthwhile tradition?

Isabella arrived at the appointed time after phoning me beforehand. With her notebook on her knees, she showered me with questions. She was very thorough, requiring explanations where necessary. I had the impression that she had adjusted extremely well to the customs and mores of this country after having been raised in Southern Europe.

A couple of weeks later she returned to verify some facts and take a photo of me.

"I'm not too keen to be photographed with my wrinkled old face. Is it really necessary?"

She insisted.

"Head and shoulders only," she suggested.

"No, no, no! Just the face and a tiny bit of the neck." And finally I selected the one which does me the least disservice.

After a cup of tea and cakes we had a long chat about what it meant to be displaced, like her, at the age of ten and the hardships her mother had to endure.

"She is a shining example to me. I want to follow in her footsteps and be as courageous as she is." She sighed. "I wonder if I will ever be as strong; no boy-friends or other distractions. The young man I was going out with had no ambition. All he wanted was a wife and children and work in an office as a minor employee from nine in the morning to five in the afternoon."

Isabella graduated a few years later with honours. A provincial paper took her on as a trainee journalist. But her aim is to write fiction. Sitting by my side, she complimented me on my selections of short stories.

"They are inspirational. I, too, have so much to tell."

"Isabella, it is not a money-maker," I warned her. "Write in your spare time; do not quit your job. Nowadays it is hard to find a publisher. You can self-publish, as I have been forced to do since my publishing firm folded; the owner had passed away. There is no guarantee you will recoup your money."

She listened to me in silence.

"Over the years I have made a profit; I recouped the money I invested and am able to save the amounts which are credited to my bank account as a result of sales on Amazon and Amazon Kindle."

Isabella heeded my advice. A provincial paper took her on as a trainee journalist. A London broadsheet editor offered her a position after a couple of years. The

urge to write fiction will never leave
her.

A Question of Class

In 'Her Sister Bella and other Stories' I described the attempts of a working class man to become socially mobile. In this selection, 'A Question of Class'; I chronicle the stark division of classes I witnessed while teaching in Harrow a few years after the last war.

Over the years I had seen her several times at bi-annual parties at the LJS, hosted by volunteers. Sally usually bakes a very rich creamy cake; every lady brings a home-baked cake which they serve before sitting down themselves. She put down the crystal dish with a couple of pieces left and pulled out the empty chair next to me.

"Help yourself to a piece and I have the last one. I'm trying to slim, unsuccessfully." Reading the name on the label pinned to my blouse, she added "Helga".

After a trivial exchange of words, the usual question cropped up.

"What did you do in your professional life, Helga?"

"I was a language teacher."

"So was I. What subjects did you teach?"

"Languages: French and German."

Sally's oval face, immaculately made-up, is arresting. Her silvery hair is drawn to the nape into a knot; in profile she has an air of an ethereal being.

She focused her dark eyes intently on me.

"And so did I, Helga." This reply led to the next question. "Where did you teach?"

"First, in 1947, in a State school in Harrow's 'posh' area. In those days most middle-class families in fully-detached houses sent their children to local schools.

Discontent started when East Enders whose houses had been damaged during the war were moved to prefabricated homes with a strip of lawn in front. Their offspring had to be admitted to local schools. The number of pupils in my class rose by twenty from one day to the next. Their knowledge was far below the required standard; their coarse speech was peppered with swear words. To silence them was very trying.

"Desks were placed in rows facing the blackboard. On the arrival of the new intake, the Head had to cope with Harrow's irate parents because their 'darlings' were now exposed to the smelly, foul-mouth East End breed.

One day a mother, fuming with rage, by-passed the school secretary and barged into the Head's office.

"My daughter has head lice. It's your fault! I demand - the other parents agree with me - that our children should be taught in another classroom, as far away as possible from that dirty mob."

He had to refuse, due to lack of staff and space, assuring her that the school nurse would inspect the children's heads regularly and would recommend a lotion to get rid of 'the pest'.

Forgetting her good manners, she shouted, "Our children have been told not to mix with the unwanted newcomers. They are not like us." With that she ran out, slamming the door behind her.

The school keeper had to move several desks towards the windows, others to the wall. This created a small gangway and separated the middle from the working class.

"I was appalled, Sally. We, the refugee children, had also been treated as inferior beings by English-Jewish parents. Most of them were descendents of Polish Jews who had migrated to London's East End at the turn of the century. So I decided to teach in Whitechapel. The evacuated population had been re-housed in block of council flats.

"During the last fifteen years of my career, I taught languages in the senior department of a school for physically handicapped pupils. These teenagers, driving themselves around the building in wheelchairs, were more committed than their fit peers. Nearly all of them were able to enrol for courses at universities, graduated and found employers willing to give them a chance.

Perhaps I learnt more from them, than they did from me about the art of living. Now in my mid-nineties, when grumbling about health-related problems I think of their patient acceptance of their fate."

"And I taught in deprived areas," she said. "We almost had to tie down our lot and push their noses into the text books. If one or two achieved high enough grades to enter university, it was the greatest reward for us."

At that point she had to resume her role as a hostess.

"We'll talk more, probably during the next party."

As so often, it has struck me that pensioners' reservoir of accumulated knowledge is completely ignored by the young. Slaves to their newfangled IT and other electronic gadgets, they are incapable of analysing and resolving problems, except for a few. If this state of affairs continues, future generations will reach maturity 'brain-dead'.

Betrayed

They first met in the hospital. Bronwen from Wales - the eldest of three younger siblings - a trained a nurse; Raymond was a junior doctor. Daily they rubbed shoulders in the paediatric ward. The ginger-haired young man admired the short girl with black curls under a white nurses' head-dress. He thought that she possessed all the qualities necessary for the care of sick children.

Both were utterly unsophisticated; their career had always been a priority. Neither of them joined fellow-students in cafes or pubs, although they were frequently invited to do so. Their single-minded commitment drew them together.

One day, both had just come off duty, Raymond took his courage in both hands. He had not dated anyone before.

"Nurse Bronwen can you possibly spare the time to have some refreshments with me in the cafe down the road?" He hesitated, "Or are you in a hurry?"

He was too shy to be seen with her in the hospital's cafeteria. His colleagues might have made fun of him behind his back or teased him unmercifully.

"No one will miss me. The other nurses are either out or snuggled up with boy-friends in the house."

Bronwen had been brought up in a small Welsh village by a strict father, a lay-preacher in Chapel. Her mother, not a disciplinarian - nor obsessed by 'God's Words' - played classical music on the upright piano, but only in her husband's absence, to the delight of her little daughter. The sheets of music were hidden from him; if he had discovered them, he would have breathed thunder and lightning. At an early age Bronwen, too, had been taught by her, as soon as the little hands could stretch over the keys of an octave.

* * *

Raymond, the only child of comfortably-off parents, still had his room in the Kensington flat. His mother and father had arrived on a *Kindertransport* with other Jewish children from Germany in 1939. After the war they were naturalized. They had benefitted from a university education which led to professional careers. By sheer chance they met again in a club frequented by former refugees and realized that they had much in common.

Raymond's piano teacher was thrilled with the talented boy.
"He reads music off the page. After he heard *Mendelsohn*'s piano concerto, he played passages from

memory. A violin might be another instrument he could learn to play."

Next day an expensive violin was purchased by his doting parents. Every evening, as soon as he had finished his homework, he practised what he had been taught; in the school orchestra he played solos on Open Days.

"He plays like *Jehudi Menhuin*", his proud mother marvelled. "My son is going to be a star; music-lovers will listen to him in the Albert Hall proms." She visualized his name in neon-lights outside concert-halls all over the world.

But Raymond, since his youth, had made up his mind to become a doctor. "It's a wonderful hobby when I want to relax, apart from the fact that musicians face an uncertain future."

His parents realized it was futile to argue with him; he was adamant.

"At university I joined the orchestra straight away. It was a welcome change from watching dead corpses being dissected," he told Bronwen.

"I was allowed to practice on the college piano in my free time; not that there was much of it. We had to 'digest mentally' so much medical knowledge and apply it when nursing patients under the vigilant eyes of the ward sister."

* * *

Their days-off and their love-making in Raymond's home came to an abrupt, unforeseen end. Expecting to see Bronwen in the morning, Matron told him the nurse had been given compassionate leave; her mother had suddenly met her end, although by then they were engaged. *Fiancés* did not qualify as a near relative of a deceased. Nor would her father, kept ignorant of his daughter's love-life, have welcomed a non-Christian future son-in-law.

Patiently he waited for her return, bombarding her with letters which she carefully hid away in her room.

Shortly after her mother's funeral Bronwen replied.

"I have given a month's notice. Dad is on his own now; my brothers live in other parts of North Wales. It is my sacred duty to be there for him, as long as he lives. I am torn in two: my love for you, darling, and my duty to him."

Raymond was incapable to deal with such a turn of events even with the steady support of his parents. Since his sheltered childhood all his wishes had been granted by his family. He felt utterly betrayed. Everyone around him tried to console him; his parents blamed themselves for his failure to get over the shock.

"There are so many other intelligent, young women who would make perfect life-partners. Try to understand Bronwen; she is making a great sacrifice to give up a happy future with you. Should one of us 'meet our Maker' you, too, would not let the surviving parent down by accepting an appointment far away from London."

He hardly listened to them.

"I am not getting married to anyone. That is it! They are all the same. I probably will indulge in the odd affair, nothing serious. I am not going to be betrayed a second time."

In his forties he became a respected part-time consultant in a children's hospital. He did not move out of the flat after both his parents had died. One of the spacious rooms he equipped for his private practice, a smaller one served as waiting room. A generous contributor and fund-raiser for research fellow-ships in childhood diseases, he became well-known in professional circles, often invited to join family celebrations by colleagues. With the help of his trusted house-keeper and her teenage daughter he was able to reciprocate. Then the flat came alive as never before. When his last visitor had left, he poured himself another drink, feeling content and relaxed.

* * *

Bronwen had been devastated to leave behind 'her golden future'. After a few months she admitted to herself that her disappointment did not diminish the joy of being back in Wales. She wandered over the hills in the fresh air and renewed the friendship with the girls she had met in her youth. She applied for a position in children's ward of a nearby hospital and, due to her excellent testimonials, was offered the job.

"Bronwen, we have to have a serious talk," her father, whose health was failing, started one evening. "I won't live forever. It is my greatest desire to see you wed."

His daughter tried to speak, but he continued. "What about your childhood sweetheart, Alun? After all these years he still yearns for you. He is thrilled that you are back with me; he is too timid to call on us."

"Dad, are you trying to be a matchmaker?"

He was not deterred. "Since his father retired, Alun and his brothers have taken over the haulage firm. He can offer you a secure future and me peace of mind. Can I have a word with him?"

"Definitely not! I am applying for a job as a district nurse which will allow me to pop in to make sure you are alright."

Her father refused to give up until she agreed to see her former boy-friend.

On meeting Alun again she discovered that, in spite of her love for Raymond, she was still fond of the cheerful, young man after more than ten years. A lonely existence was abhorrent to her; she answered 'yes' after he had proposed.

Everyone crammed into the chapel to be present at the ceremony conducted by her father. Once the guests had left the reception, Alun told her, "I am really not that religious. I only pay lip-service when I pray."

That was a great relief to Bronwen. "And I only go with my father to Chapel to please him."

They moved in with him; he was wasting away, repeating over and over again, "I do miss your mother. I don't want to carry on without her."

No medication would assuage his grief before his death.

Alun was not as strong as his younger siblings. The eldest, he strove to work even harder than them.

"You will exhaust yourself," his wife warned when he staggered home, preferring to walk and breathe in fresh air after the fumes he had inhaled in the garage. At her insistence he did the paperwork in the office rather than repair large vehicles.

Near to despair, they had to accept they were denied parenthood. Bronwen assumed that her husband was 'the guilty party'; she did not raise the issue with him or suggest fertility treatment. Instead, they spoilt their many nieces and nephews, although it got them into trouble with sisters-in-law. But the children adored their aunt and uncle; whenever possible, they went to their house to devour the cakes and other goodies on the front-room table. After tea they rushed upstairs to 'their room' to play with the toys which had been bought for them.

Day in day out Bronwen watched Alun like a hawk. To reach the office he had to climb up a narrow flight of stairs. The effort made him cough and damaged his lungs. It alarmed her.

"I must have caught a chill. Don't make a mountain out of a mole-hill," he joked.

He was wrong. Bronwen had to drag him to the doctor. An X-ray confirmed her worst fears. Alun had tuberculosis at an advanced stage. He coughed up more and more blood; there was no 'miracle cure'.

* * *

After the funeral, gutted, she longed for a change - perhaps, going back to London and tie up loose ends. Was Raymond still single or married?

"Of course, everything fell into his lap since childhood. No wonder he felt betrayed," she thought.

To be on the safe side she contacted a former, older nursing colleague who wrote back, "Raymond is not married. He is a senior part-time consultant in the children's hospital. To anyone who cares to listen he explains that he will never marry because he has been betrayed, "and I quote his very words, 'My faith in the fidelity of women has been so shaken that I will remain single all my life.'

"Bronwen, it would be a mistake to come back to London in the hope you can rekindle his love, however much we miss you."

After re-reading the letter several times she went to bed. "A good night's rest will do me a world of good," she felt.

But she was plagued by harrowing dreams, one of them more vivid than the others:

She had not heeded the advice, quit her job after four weeks' notice and drove to London. The shortage of nurses was acute; soon she had started to work in the children's hospital. From the distance she spotted Raymond in the long corridors, surrounded by students and staff. The sight of him woke her; for a few seconds she sat rigid in bed, then fell back again like in a trance. Now she was standing by the door in the hospital's cafeteria. She saw a distorted vision of him, alone, at a table. Again she woke up - out of breath - seconds later the nightmare continued. Absorbed in a medical journal, he did not notice she was approaching, or that she had settled down opposite him.

Her throat was dry; she hissed "Raymond." He stared at her with glassy eyes like a ghost. This made her shiver and she shot upright, throwing the blankets on the floor.

"It's a dream," she screamed, trying to rouse herself. In vain! The nightmare had her in its grip. The bloodless lips in Raymond's white face twisted and, in a primeval voice, he uttered, "betrayed, betrayed," pointing his skeletal finger towards her.

Soaked in sweat, she cried out so loudly that it woke her up completely.

* * *

Bronwen was passionate about her work, exhilarated when driving through the familiar countryside. She met anxious parents, worried about their children, who expressed their gratitude in words and gifts. Through one couple she learned that the musical director of the amateur orchestra had been searching for a pianist. She got in touch with him. After a short audition she started rehearsing with the other musicians.

"Some of us go on hikes on Saturday, if we have no engagements. You seem fit enough to keep up with the toughest of our group. Why not join us? Wear boots when we go up Snowdon," a violinist told her.

Stiff at first, her limbs soon limbered up; she kept pace with the interesting people who had come into her life. Still not yet fifty, full of vigour, Bronwen was satisfied with her existence. Except for a few grey hairs and more grooves in her face, she had not much changed in the past two decades. Her pleasant nature and demeanour still attracted men, especially widowers, who wanted to marry her. And after all those years she still could not figure out why Raymond had felt betrayed? Did it bother her? No, not any more.

"I have friends I can count on, a wonderful career. I have no regrets and need nothing else."

In this vein she carried on to a ripe old age, finding pleasure in all her past-times. Having reached her mid-eighties, reclining in her Dad's old armchair, her mind travelled through the chapters of her life. "I am certain," she said to herself, "there is no one who crossed my path whom I have wilfully betrayed."

The Hoaxer

"There is no fool, like an old fool", so the saying goes.

Recently I have joined the ranks with the best of them, in spite of warnings in the media and Internet.

Caught completely unawares while immersed in the realm of fiction, I was an easy prey for the soft, oriental voice on the phone. I could not hear or understand him clearly; my alarm bells switched on 'mute'.

"I am ringing from BT. We are going to disconnect you."

"What do you mean? No Internet, no word - processing?"

"That's right. We are disconnecting you within the next ten minutes," he stated in a foreign accent.

Not trusting whether I had heard him correctly, I asked him to repeat his words. He cleared his throat and in a more precise tone reiterated the unpleasant news.

"Why?" I was aghast. "Everything is functioning perfectly well."

"There are certain changes we have to make," he went on, "that's why we are shutting all customers down."

"No, no, no," I yelled through the line. "I must not lose a connection; I am a published writer."

"Oh! Under what name?"

"Helga Wolff. You can find my titles on Amazon."

After a few minutes silence, "I can see them; nice covers. Congratulations!"

A string of five syllables were too difficult for him to pronounce; I asked, "What did you say?"

"Con-gra-tu-la-tions."

Was he going to buy a book, crossed my mind?

"What is the first one about?"

And, like a lamb led to slaughter, I answered, "It's an autobiography, the story of my life."

This opened a Pandora box of questions, and I fell hook, line and sinker by revealing details on the phone to him, a complete stranger - possibly residing in a far distant country - facts not included in the book which should have been kept secret.

To mention my high age was the most idiotic mistake. However, it was his response which finally woke me up to the danger I was courting.

"What a wonderful age! Are you living by yourself?"

The fool could at least have disguised his intentions more effectively.

"My family live within ear-shot, my good friends next door and another helpful couple down the road."

"Ear-shot?" A new word for his limited vocabulary.

"Very, very close and on call day and night," I paraphrased. With a firm voice, "The door-bell is ringing."

"I can wait."

This was getting out of hand. I had lost my patience and finished off. "I have nothing else to say. If you phone again, I will ask the police to trace your call. You are either a cold-caller or, worse, a hoaxer." And I put the receiver down.

That incident occurred a few months ago. I was ashamed of my failure to identify that he was an 'unseen, vocal intruder'. The lesson has been learnt!

Neighbourliness

The names have slipped my mind; I have given them fictitious names: Brenda and Ralph. They used to live in a semi facing the road which leads to the well-kept local park. On sunny days we would see the plump, short woman in her sixties chatting to people next door. At first we just nodded or said "hello". Soon she made us stop with an engaging smile on her round face framed by curly, brown hair, though she had just turned sixty.

"You moved into the house opposite the library not long ago. I have seen you in the shops. You seem to have settled in very quickly. Do you like it round here?"

"Oh yes. It's just right for us now; enough rooms for the two of us and our daughter when she comes home from Bristol. The supermarkets nearby stock everything we need. Hopefully, we will not have to depend on them for a while. My husband still drives us to Sainsbury and Asda; there is much more choice and it is cheaper."

That was over forty years ago. Gradually we got to know one another better until, one afternoon, she said,

"Come and have tea with us and meet Ralph, my husband. His business takes him often abroad. Sometimes I used to accompany him. Now my 'travelling days' are long over. I don't want to sleep in a strange bed."

It surprised me and made me laugh; in our mid-fifties we were still keen to explore other countries in Europe.

" 'My home is my castle'. Ralph will carry on for another four years until his retirement. I am looking forward to a long old age together and to not being separated from him so often."

It was delightful to be with Ralph. He was amusing and regaled us with anecdotes about his colleagues and business contacts abroad.

"One Englishman prefers to share a flat with his French mistress, *Françoise*, than be with his wife who does not know about her. *Françoise* believes he is a bachelor who will one day marry her. With this arrangement he has kept his marriage intact."

* * *

A few months later my late husband was hospitalized. Even without being asked, Brenda offered to drive me to see him and to supermarkets.

We were in the cafeteria when she opened up. "Ralph and I have two daughters in their mid-thirties. One is married with two kids, the other is single. Ralph loves our grandchildren and gets on well with his son-in-law. The other was a teen-age monster. She would not listen to us, to her teachers or her sister. And when she told us she is gay there was an unholy row. Ralph threw her out when she earned enough money to be independent. That was over ten years ago. She rings me frequently. When I put the phone down, she knows her intolerant father is at home.

It makes no difference to me that she lives with her girl-friend, as long as she is healthy and happy."

How very sad. We were careful never to mention her in his presence.

* * *

Ten years later Ralph came towards us outside our house; his gait was like a sleep-walker's. His face was empty of expression, his back humped and his grey hair was dishevelled.

"Are you alright? Come inside and have a cup of tea?" We were worried seeing him in such a state.

He did not respond, passed by us and ambled on towards the corner of the street. Back in our sitting room we rang Brenda.

"Is he wandering aimlessly about again?" I heard her deep sigh. "I'll catch up with him and coax him back home."

Shortly afterwards we saw her, still in her apron, her hair in disarray, rushing after him, her broad, heavy body heaving to catch her breath. A few minutes later we watched her leading him back.

Alzheimers was diagnosed; his mental faculties disintegrated rapidly. His wife desperately wanted to keep him in his familiar surroundings. Her married daughter tied down by a job and domestic duties could not be counted on. She did not dare to accept her single daughter's help, worried he might react violently. There was no other choice: Ralph had to be institutionalized.

Heart-broken to be without him, she fell down the stairs. Her legs, always swollen, even when she was fit, had to be put into plaster. It was impossible for her to stay in her home. Her daughter took her in.

Brenda hoped, once the plaster had been removed, she would be able to return. She was wrong. Owing to lack of movement she had put on more weight; the legs refused to support her heavy frame. A wheelchair had to be provided for her. She could not attend the funeral when Ralph had passed away. Owing to an increasing number of other medical problems she could not safely be taken out. This and all the other disasters which had befallen her broke her spirits.

One morning when her daughter brought Brenda a cup of tea she found her dead on the floor. It was assumed that she had rolled out of bed during the night. The autopsy revealed that a heart attack after the fall had killed her.

When I pass the house, where she had been married and had raised her daughters, I remember her smiling face, her gregariousness as she stood at the gate, always eager to engage neighbours in a conversation.

The house must have been sold to an absentee owner and is in the hands of estate agents. The exterior usually gets a face lift before a 'To Let' sign has been placed on the drive.

Fanatics

Harald, my German friend and mentor, suggested over the phone, "Why don't you write a piece about fanatics, those of the middle of the twentieth century and the more recent crop, whose twisted minds cause destruction and deaths not just in Europe, but world-wide."

* * *

In Hitler's Third Reich there existed clear demarcation lines between Arians with at least three generations of Christian blood flowing in their veins and the non-Aryans whose blood had been tainted: Jews, homosexuals and the deformed. These innocents were rounded up, deported. They perished in the Holocaust; a minority were used as guinea pigs in the clinic of Dr. Mengele.

The average German citizens, concerned with their family's wellbeing and the future of the children, gradually fell in with the regime, distancing themselves from the introduction of the racial laws in the privacy of their homes. Had they dared to speak out, they were likely to share the fate of the unwanted, disenfranchised, incarcerated victims.

An eerie kind of certainty existed: one knew whom to trust, who was one's friend and who was the enemy. The Jewish community closed ranks. Even those who had never been religious sought comfort in synagogues.The number of congregants exceeded the expectation of the rabbis.

Children of school-age were banned from state schools. I had been separated from my peers, the girls with whom I had grown up. Jews were forbidden to handle Aryan books. My father's university bookshop folded, so did the

Antiquariat near the Goethe House where foreign and old titles could be purchased. To clear his debts, mahogany furniture and precious first editions had to be sold. From our spacious five-room apartment we moved into a top-floor flat. My parents' finances reached the lowest ebb some time later; two of the four rooms were let to a couple of ladies, musicians in the Jewish orchestra. (Their contracts with the town's symphony orchestra had been ended, not due to lack of talent but because of their faith.)

To make ends meet my mother worked as a carer. She helped an old lady mornings and evenings. It was a balancing act to fit in her house-wifely duties: cooking for the four of us and keeping the place clean. Without contributions from my maternal relatives in Berlin we would have been in great trouble, like many others who were unable to find a safe haven abroad.

It was frightening to pass posters with *Juden raus* or *Juden unerwünscht* ('out with the Jews' or 'Jews unwanted') as I rode on my bicycle to school. When I saw Nazis strutting about in their brown uniforms near the house. I was frightened, fearing that my father and brother, then a seventeen-year-old, would be arrested.

My father and brother were sent to a concentration camp in 1939. My parent returned thin as a skeleton; my sibling had been recruited by a Bolivian to work in the mines. I guess the Germans were glad to get rid of as many of the inmates as possible. I wonder if this was a lucrative business for camp commanders: one human being sold for cash, like slaves in the olden days.

* * *

Now, in the twenty-first century, we are threatened all over the world by another enemy, the suicide-bomber. He lets loose his weapons in crowds who enjoy themselves in their leisure pursuits or he targets a particular person or section of a community. In their houses they manufacture explosives, unbeknown to the neighbours. Parents in some cases have been horrified, unaware of their offspring's activities. Religious Muslim leaders have condemned their co-religionists who, contrary to the Koran, wilfully annihilate the Infidel. They blame Imams who radicalize the young by their sermons in the mosque. This country prides itself for its FREEDOM OF SPEECH, but where should a line be drawn?

Going out and about my *fief*, Wembley, I notice many young Muslims wearing their caps the wrong way round, in tee-shirts and jeans, laughing, full of fun. They are probably also categorised as Infidels by the fanatics whose existence is shadowed by gloom and doom.

On the 14th of June a fire broke out in a tower-block in Kensington at one o'clock in the morning. It killed residents who were trapped, fatally injuring others and the survivors traumatised and homeless. The fanatics probably deem this inferno to have been inflicted to them by Allah, an unchallengeable proof that he is on THEIR SIDE.

* * *

In the last decade of the twentieth century I witnessed 'a less vicious expression' of fanaticism in the train from Mainz to Frankfurt. Workers from the East had flooded into Germany and were employed in factories. They usually kept themselves to themselves, except Sundays when they ventured into the big city.

Two *Gastarbeiter* ('guest workers') sat down on empty seats next to a *bourgeoise*, well-dressed German lady. She forgot her manners, pulled a face and got up to find a free place, not polluted by Easterners. Is that the right way to treat 'guests'? Nor was she the only one who looked down on the Eastern labour force. They were partly responsible for creating the *Wirtschaftswunder* (the economic miracle) of the defeated nation which rose again, like 'a Phoenix from the ashes', to become the greatest power in the European Union.

Vichy

The very word sends shivers down my spine! Had Providence not been on my side, I would have remained in Paris with my aunt after the outbreak of WWII, accompanied her and my uncle to *La Zone Libre*, governed by Maréchal Pétain. *La Zone* was not really *libre*; he was beholden to the Germans even before they occupied the last part of France.

My relations, Wally and Jas, managed to get to Switzerland before the 'Jackboots' took total control. Their money was hidden in the seams of aunt's dresses. At the frontier half of it was confiscated by soldiers. Jas, not as tough as his Catholic-born wife, collapsed and passed away before she returned home to Paris. The *concierge*, a wily old woman, greeted her, "*Les Boches ont pris tout.*" (The Germans had confiscated the flat; before leaving had stolen anything of value.)

I visited Wally in 1947. She had rebuilt her fashion business on a smaller scale, sublet two rooms. Her resilience and courage were boundless.

* * *

In the claustrophobic atmosphere of a police cell prisoners sat on a wooden bench; they were trembling while they waited to be examined by the short, stocky doctor in a white overall. "It was just a job," he would swear at the Nürenberg Tribunals, pleading his innocence.

One by one they were taken out of sight by a German in brown uniform. If they had been circumcised, their fate was sealed. A hollow thud announced they had been disposed of, like the *aristocrates* who were beheaded by the *guillotine* during the French Revolution.

The play was a stark reminder of what could have happened to me. When danger loomed on the political horizon, nuns in *La Zone Libre* hid Jewish children in their orphanage. I could have been one of them.

The youngsters were told to be as quiet as mice when soldiers were marching nearby. The Sisters respected that they had been brought up in the Jewish faith, though a few among them, out of gratitude to their saviours, became converts when they had reached adulthood.

Collaborateurs, to gain favours with the invader, betrayed the pious nuns. They were deported with the children; some were only five years old. Almost all of them perished in the death camp.

* * *

For decades I had not given any thought as to what might have happened to me after The Fall of

France. Mesmerised, I watched the tragedy; the harrowing past surfaced into my consciousness, as it unrolled in front of my eyes. The impact it has made on me is unlike any other play I had ever seen before. 'Vichy' has taken hold of my imagination: the history of racism in the twentieth and twenty-first centuries in France makes me shudder.

The French Revolution in 1789 was supposed to herald 'A Golden Age' of *Liberté*, *Egalité* and *Fraternité*. Jews had been granted full citizenship in 1791. However they were barred from many professions until 1831. In the years from 1936 to 1938 Léon Blum was at the helm of government. But the ideal of a pluralistic society was abandoned in Vichy: France must be *judenrein* (free of Jews).

Blum was imprisoned, but survived the concentration camp, and now, neo- Nazis, still in thrall of Vichy's persecution of the Jews, object to the government's inclusiveness policy, objecting that their rallies have been outlawed.

L'Affaire Dreyfus - the army captain wrongfully accused of treason in 1894 until he was exonerated in 1906 - is so typical of what was to follow in the future. Racists spread it about that, "French Jews are more loyal to Israel than to France", and "They have too much power in the business world". There are those who deny the Holocaust. Le Pen's National Front is at the fore-front of spreading anti-Semitic propaganda, though at the moment the party singles out Algerians and other naturalized people from former colonies in North Africa.

There have been recent incidents in this country as well, but not on such a large scale. I was shocked when I was downloading some of the facts below.

Jan. 2015: "Kosher supermarket siege, Porte de Vincennes."
Feb: "Soldiers guarding Jewish community centre in Nice attacked."
Oct: "Three Jews attacked outside synagogue in Marseilles."
Nov: "Jewish teacher stabbed in Marseilles."
Jan. 2016: "Jewish teacher attacked."
Aug: "A sixty-two-year old Jew attacked in Strasbourg."
April 2017: "Orthodox Jewess attacked in Paris."

Many of the hate-crimes have been committed by French subjects of Algerian descent, indoctrinated by vociferous Imams or Isis supporters. The failure to solve the Israeli-Palestinian question is invariably cited as the cause. They, as well as Anti-Semites, now side-lined by the State, recall with satisfaction that Jews were eliminated in Vichy during WWII.

Yet, lately, the rise of Anti-Semitism is believed to be a more general attitude towards the Jewish population. In his recent speech the French President, Emanuel Macron, has apologized to the Jewish community for what happened to them during the Occupation of France. This has not prevented the exodus to Israel which has topped 6000, or the large number of families now settled in London. A French friend of mine, mother of two teenagers, has not yet given up her flat in Paris. "It will blow over," she assures me.

"It cannot last. It will blow over," my father, always an optimist, prophesized when Hitler's harsh racial laws wrecked the German Jewish community. History proved that it did not 'blow over', nor will the negative attitude towards their Jewish countrymen in France. Vichy and its scenario of institutionalized hatred has won!

Narcissa
(A female Narcissus)

Like Narcissus, son of the Greek mythological river god, Cephissus, Angela was bewitched by the reflection of herself in the long mirror. She stood in front of it in the narrow space changing the style of her hair and her make-up before going out and on her return. It annoyed her mother when she tried to manoeuvre the shopping trolley past her in the hall and her father when he came back after a hard day's work.

"She wastes her time admiring herself," or "she is just idling her life away." Both worried themselves sick, fearing the worst about her future.

* * *

"Tomasz is back again on Sunday," my friend and neighbour told me. Sure enough, I saw him on Tuesday in the garden next door and waved.

Almost a decade ago he had rented John's house for about fifteen years. "I do want to see my children grow up." His face was pitiful to behold. "But there is not much work for us builders in Poland. Here I can earn enough for my keep, send money home and employ others on a temporary basis if I need them. They are quite happy to be here, make some money and then get back to their families again; I am the one who is stuck in London."

While he and his colleagues were in residence, one of the young men's sisters, Sylvia, came to study English before qualifying as a beautician. One Saturday night the usually very quiet builders threw a party. It was her twenty-first birthday. Hell broke loose. My late husband phoned. No answer. The noise had drowned the ringing sound. He rang the door-bell. No answer. The increasing volume of carousing could not be penetrated.

Exasperated, he ran to the garden fence. He shouted and shouted until he was practically hoarse.

"Right! If no one bothers to come out I will call the police. This is intolerable; it's after eleven o'clock."

He was just on the point of walking towards our sitting room's patio door when a young Indian appeared with a can of beer. He was drunk; he stared at us with a silly smile on his face. A lovely, blonde young girl rushed towards him.

"I am so sorry you have been disturbed. Subhash has just proposed to me on his bended knees. I said I would marry him. It has gone to his head because he says that he is madly in love with me."

On Sunday Tomasz and one of his colleagues came to apologize. "What was to be a civilized party got out of hand. As a matter of fact we had to throw out one of the boys because he had started a quarrel for no reason whatsoever; he became violent. I promise it won't happen again." And it did not.

* * *

We invited Sylvia for tea to show that there were no ill-feelings. She was delighted to be friends and was very expansive.

"I am working shifts in the kiosk at Kilburn Station. I am managing it!" She giggled. "It's only just me there; the supervisor who checks the takings trusts me, so I feel I am in charge."

We were surprised that her English was so fluent; her accent was very strong.

"A young, good-looking Indian came every morning to buy a newspaper as regularly as clockwork before catching a train. A month or so later he started arriving much earlier than usual and stopped to 'chat me up', as my English girl-friend said. He asked me out. Well, I realized that I love him. That's why he behaved like crazy!"

"Aren't you going back to finish your studies?"

"Oh that! It really doesn't matter anymore. My future is with him and our children and..."

I interrupted her enthusiastic flow of words. "A word of warning, young lady: It all sounds wonderful and I hope all your wishes will come true. But who can foretell the future? If I were you, I would go back to Poland, finish your studies and get your certificate or diploma."

"And what about Subhash?"

"If he really loves you, he will wait," I assured her.

She followed my advice implicitly. They married two years later, as soon as he was a qualified engineer and earned enough to keep her.

* * *

On Sundays the couple had lunch next door. Invariably Sylvia popped in to see me. Nine months after the wedding day her baby boy was born. They celebrated in style after he had been christened in London's Polish church, but they kept the noise down.

"Sahib will be both: Catholic and Hindu. That's what we have decided. In summer we will show him off to Subhash's parents in Bombay," she said; she was dressed in a beautiful sari.

"It suits you, Sylvia. They will be delighted to see."

"Subhash promised to buy others for me in India. His mother has good taste and will help me choose the right garments. I can't wait. It is all so exciting. Who would have thought that a Polish girl from a small town would travel half way round the world. It's like a dream."

She was 'on a high'. I refrained from discouraging her with what was on my mind. How would she communicate with her in-laws who only spoke rudimentary English. Having anticipated my question, she remarked, "They will be relieved that their son, wild in his youth, has settled down and will adore their first grandchild. Above all, they will be relieved that he will be a Hindu."

On her return she told me that she had been accepted by her husband's very large family and that she was pregnant again.

"It's good to have another baby so soon after Sahib's birth and it is a GIRL," she emphasized. "That's enough. No other children so we can do the best for two."

The flat was too small to accommodate a family of four. To buy a house in this area was beyond their means, especially with additional expenses after the baby was born. She was baptised Angela. "A Christian name and a Hindu name; we embrace all," Sylvia said. "I can't even pass on the clothes Sahib has grown out of to Angela. All has to be new. Never mind, somehow we will manage."

Neither Sylvia nor her husband had the slightest idea that the little infant would be a 'Narcissa'.

They bought a small property in Watford's less affluent area and moved away soon afterwards. She never forgot to knock on our front door when she visited her brother and showed off her baby in the carry-cot. Sylvia doted on the rosy-cheeked blond little one with olive skin who resembled her.

"Angela will be a beauty. You will have to keep all her admirers at bay." She smiled. "Perhaps she will marry a rich man and won't have to turn over every penny like we do."

* * *

Sahib was very bright. I remember how as an eleven-year-old he questioned me while he studied the pictures on the sitting room wall. His thirst for knowledge was boundless. When my answers did not satisfy him, he downloaded information from the internet. He won a scholarship at Eton, went to Cambridge and graduated with first-class honours. After working for an art dealer for several years he became an authenticator of Flemish paintings. The canvasses belonged to people who were either just keen to know their value or to families who needed to sell their precious possessions due to financial hardship.

Angela, an attractive eighteen-year-old, had no idea what she wanted to do in the future. Her parents hoped she would go to university. She was not studious, though highly intelligent. Her parents were desperate. "All your former classmates have either gone on to higher education or have found jobs.

We are fed up with the way you carry on. We have decided to stop your pocket money in a couple of weeks. If you are still gallivanting around then, eyeing new outfits in shop windows, you won't be able to afford them."

Their daughter shrugged her shoulders in defiance, felt misunderstood, bolted out of the room, slamming the door behind her. It upset them and they began to ask themselves where they went wrong.

"We have brought our children up in two cultures. Our son was able to cope with his two identities; she is not. Most likely she is not even aware of this. It's our fault," Sylvia, her mother, always was at pains to find excuses.

"Nonsense! For once let us stick to our ultimatum." Her father was firm; his wife knew no argument would soften him.

Next day, going shopping with her mother, Angela stopped in front of the local hairdressers' salon to look at the photographs of models with the latest hair styles. No doubt she was deciding which one would suit her best.

Her mother, though, was more interested in the card stuck to the inside of the window. She pointed to it. "Look, Angela, they require an apprentice and they will even pay you the minimum wage while you are learning the trade. Shall I make some enquiries?"

The threat of losing her pocket money had galvanised her daughter.

"No. I will go in and apply. I want to handle it myself, Mummy. Sit in the cafe opposite and wait for me."

This unexpected, positive response delighted her mother.

Half-an-hour later, her face radiant, Angela sat down beside her. With a jubilant voice she announced, "The manageress has taken me on, Mummy. The apprenticeship is about three years. I promise I will persevere."

"At last, there is a beginning", said Sylvia to her husband that night.

* * *

At first Angela was only allowed to shampoo clients' hair. When Mrs. Clark, the manageress, promoted her to the next step, drying hair, she watched as her apprentice surreptitiously experimented which styles would enhance the client's looks.

"You are a talented girl and you learn very quickly, copying your senior colleagues. You will do well." Mrs. Clark's encouraging words thrilled the young girl; she could hardly wait to repeat them to her parents in the evening.

The three years passed more quickly than she had anticipated. After receiving the official certificate which was displayed on the wall with the others, Mrs. Clark's proposal seemed to Sylvia like the best birthday present she had ever received. "I offer you a junior partnership. The head office wants to move you to the West End. To be quite honest, I do not want to lose you."

"I am staying with you and I want to carry on making all our local ladies look as beautiful as possible."

And soon, on the recommendation of these local ladies, clients from neighbouring areas increased the number of the clientele.

When Mrs. Clark retired, Angela stepped into her shoes with a vastly increased salary as the takings of the salon had more than tripled.

No more did she indulge in 'window-shopping'. She was able to buy whatever she fancied to her heart's content and be stirred by her beauty as she stood in front of the long mirror, like the mythological Greek god Narcissus.

Errors of Judgment

Once again I needed the temporary help of a qualified carer or nurse in the absence of my exceptionally compassionate carer, Sunitha, who was recovering after surgery. Suffering from vertigo, I had broken three toes of my right foot trying to prevent a fall and causing more serious damage to my head. After an X-Ray at the local hospital's A and E department the doctor advised me to wear a Velcro boot for six weeks until the toes had healed.

It weighed like a ton with the heavy raised sole. That same evening as I was trying to take 'the monster' off I was at a loss how to do so, blaming myself for not having watched the therapist when he fitted my foot into it. For almost half-an-hour I struggled to undo the Velcro strips with my arthritic hands and to manoeuvre the foot out of the boot. There was no one else about, so I had to get on with it.

Recovering from the ordeal I now waddle like a duck. It makes me self-conscious. When I recall my ninety-year old my mother-in-law's wise words, now that I am in the mid-nineties, "Who do you think looks at you", I cannot help but smile.

Rather than finding a replacement for Sunitha via a carer's agency, I preferred a carer who worked on a private basis. A friend recommended Hedda. As soon as I had exchanged a few words with her on the phone, we 'clicked'. However, due to her previous commitments, Chandra, an NHS nurse, filled the gap.

Over a period of ten days it was a litany of trial and error with her. To cram into one hour my personal needs: in the shower, dress me, prepare breakfast, a lunch-time meal and sandwiches for supper - caused both of us to be pressurized. She was so short with me, that I became a nervous wreck.

Enough, is enough! I geared myself as she was in mid-flight on her way out.

"I am an old, vulnerable woman, please treat me more gently."

She was outraged. "Some of my patients are older than you. I have never had any issue with them."

"Perhaps I am more sensitive than they are. Please take on board what I said."

After she had left I wondered if she would give up on me. But I did not regret that I had stood my ground, though I decided to turn over a new leaf and outline sketch my past were she to turn up again. It worked wonders.

"I admire the way you are positive in spite of being incapacitated."

From that moment onwards she treated me more sympathetically, yet keeping an eye on her wrist watch.

* * *

My greatest error of judgment concerned a willowy, beautiful Jamaican called Hedda, whose looks belied her fifty-seven years. Black curly hair parted in the middle, and hanging down to her neck. Possibly, before slavery was abolished, one of her female ancestors was raped by a white overseer or sugar plantation owner. Hence the light brown colour of her skin. A devout Christian, she went to church every Sunday after being with me.

Hedda went 'by the book' after private tuition for professional carers.

"The short inadequate training given by carers agencies is useless."

I agreed whole-heartedly, because I spoke from experiencing it myself. The young woman had never before 'cared' for a white person.

"We are all the same: white or coloured," I assured her. She was never comfortable with me.

On the days Hedda had to no other patient - the official word is 'client' - she described her family life back home.

"Younger people look after the older generation and appreciate their wisdom and experience."

In the West any one over sixty is considered to be out of touch with the present, in fact *passé*. Parents and grandparents occupy the third or fourth place in their offspring's programs. In some families children are not even in contact with them; their existence is practically ignored.

"What a bad example you are for your children. One day you, too, will be old," I would like to warn them. "They will behave like you did; you will be neglected and lonely."

* * *

"When I retire I will return to Jamaica to my family. That's where I belong. All of us look after each other and the children of younger mothers. Most of the men-folk are absent; they usually contribute little or nothing financially for the upbringing of their youngsters. We live happily together without them. No, we are better off without them."

"And what about your son and daughter?" Her views were so alien to me. "You are going to leave them behind? I couldn't bear to be too far away from my daughter and her family. To be in contact by phone or mobile would not satisfy me."

"Since they were born I gave my two everything they needed. I looked after them while they were at school, contributed towards the rent while they were at university and made sure they had enough money not only to feed themselves but also to enjoy leisure pursuits. I worked long hours to be able to do so. Now they are in their mid-thirties with good jobs. It's up to them to steer their ship."

She was adamant, convinced that she was right.

"I have been a good mother," she said again. "MY turn has come. So I go back to my roots, surrounded by my large family, like it is the custom in Jamaica."

"Wouldn't you like to see your grandchildren grow up? Every time my family visits me I am overjoyed."

"Not really. If they want to see me, they know where I am. But I have made it clear to them that the properties I own in Jamaica will not be passed down to them. They will be sold to secure my old age."

I was left speechless.

* * *

I celebrated my birthday a week before her last day with me. When I came downstairs a vase full of flowers greeted me. She had picked them in her garden in the morning. A card for 'Nana' was propped up against them.

"We call grandmothers 'nana' in Jamaica," she explained.

I was truly overwhelmed and completely taken aback by Hedda's sincerity. That was the beginning of a wonderful day, followed by a delicious lunch by my friends next door. I was moved that Grace had somehow elicited my favourite dishes from me.

A week later, Hedda sent me an e-mail, enquiring about my wellbeing. She had attached photos she had taken of the flowers. I have photo-copied one; I am now using it on greeting cards.

Down Memory Lane

Every day, perched on a pressure cushion, I travel downstairs with the stair lift. The pictures on the wall, like a memory-lane, record the many places my late husband and I visited: first with our daughter in tandem, later just the two of us during our long and happy marriage.

1 Rome: The Vatican

In the middle, flanked by others, The Vatican takes pride of place on the wall of the hall. The morning we entered the Basilica we were fascinated by the shaft of sunlight which illuminated Michael Angelo's gilded dome. It nearly blinded us.

Outside the Swiss Guards, parading in mediaeval livery, is a constant attraction to sightseers. It was not one of the days when the Pope blesses the faithful.

I could not help remembering that, during The Third Reich, Pius XII kept '*stumm*' when Hitler's regime persecuted Jews, non-Aryans and other 'vermin' who perished in the death camps. Was he truly following the Ten Commandments during The Final Solution or was he, like so many politicians, being pragmatic? "We don't want to ruffle feathers", or, "It's in the national interest."

The Allied Powers condemned him. According to them, he was a Nazi sympathiser. Others claim the Pope had been unfairly judged because thousands of Jews were hidden in churches on his orders.

2 Italy: Florence

The sun spreads its rays over the cloudy sky-line. The golden dome of the Basilica dwarfs all other nearby buildings. At lunch time we walked through the narrow streets to find a restaurant frequented by Italians. The one in the square charged an exorbitant price for the small cups of coffee which the waiter served. But it was worth it: Michelangelo's sculpture of David was facing us.

3 Greece: Delphi

Our daughter photographed the Dorian columns at the entrance of the temple. Climbing up the slope, we saw the amphitheatre where athletes wrestled during the first Olympic Games. But what caught my imagination was the rock on which the Oracle sat predicting the future. The legend tells us, she was endowed with special powers. She is the predecessor of all the soothsayers, mediums - in my estimation charlatans - who consider themselves qualified to foretell the future or call up the ghosts of the departed, mostly for cash. They exploit the vulnerable, unable to cope with grief.

4 North Wales

Outside our hotel in Bet-sy-Coed the water rushes over boulders after rainfall. I stood alone on the bridge, fascinated by the foaming stream and the hissing waves. An episode of vertigo overtook me. My hands failed to grip the rails. When George found me I was slumped on the ground, surrounded by gesticulating people.

"I pushed through them and nearly had a heart attack when I saw your white face," he said after he had managed to get me round and had piloted me to the cafe by the railway line. "What do you think triggered it?"

"My senses of sight and hearing must have become 'unhinged' while I was staring down below."

After that he did not leave me on my own during our holidays.

5 Berlin

Das Brandenburger Tor, a neo-classical monument, erected in the 18th century, is Berlin's most famous landmark. During the Cold War it divided the capital into two separate states: Democratic West and Communist East. It was then that I visited Berlin again.

As a child I used to spend my holidays with my grandmother, uncle and aunts in their flat in the *Schlüterstrasse*. With my cousin I had freely wandered through the capital.

That was not possible any more. A bus took us to the East. The blocks of flats built after the end of hostilities looked like barracks, not fit to house the civilian population. Through the window of the bus, we were not allowed to get off, we peered at the down-trodden people in drab clothes. They peered at the 'rich' passengers; two classes eyeing each other.

* * *

 Subsequently we flew many times to Berlin. From the terrace outside one of the cafes on the *Kurfüstendamm* we watched 'the world go by'. Nothing much had changed. Elderly patrons chatted together, consuming pastries, just as they did before the war. Opposite people from the East were drawn towards shop windows, overwhelmed by the expensive jewellery and the latest fashion. None of them went inside. They could not afford to buy anything.

6 The Cotswolds

It was a glorious autumn; the leaves of Burford's high street were just beginning to shed their golden leaves. We passed by the church and houses, built in the unique style of the area with Tudor and Georgian shop fronts.

At the far end of the street the souvenir shop was selling mugs. We bought one with our daughter's name on it. She drank out of it for years until one of us carelessly had dropped it. Liquid escaped out of the hair-line crack.

I was just about to bin it.

"No", she cried. "I want to keep it on my chest of drawers." It is still there after more than forty decades.

The Staircase Wall

Six prints line the staircase walls: German Medieval knights (*Landsknechte*) in armour, one with a drum, another with a pipe and the third carries a flag, are marching towards their destination. Four other prints depict medieval towns. They are signed.

I took them out of the frames and sent them to a German friend. We both were under the impression that they were priceless treasures which I could sell if I were 'skinned'. We were wrong; they did not rate much in the eyes of the auctioneer.

I inherited them from my mother-in-law. She valued them highly. I can imagine how disappointed she would have been if, like in the TV series 'Fake or Fortune', they would not have been authenticated by an expert. Nevertheless, they mean much to me, beyond price.

In their midst, in a long oblong frame, bought in Berlin, all the famous buildings, East and West which had been damaged by bombs during the last war, are represented.

Right at the top of the stairs, lit by the window at the side, hangs my late friend's 'Daffodils'. This is one of Evelyn's beautiful paintings which remind me of our long friendship and our walks in The Lakes through fields of yellow daffodils during our student days.

Yom Kippur

Today, the 29th September 2017 (the 10th *Tishri*5777 according to the Jewish calendar), Jews all over the world congregate in synagogues to participate in the Yom Kippur service. When I was a three-year-old my mother put me next to her in the Liberal Synagogue in Frankfurt-on-Main's West End. While we were sitting down some air reached me; standing up I was dwarfed by over-dressed women around us. The vapours of their perfumes - mostly Chanel, as in those days the West End community in Frankfurt was well off - almost anaesthetized me. Once, my anxious mother took me home before the end of the morning service.

Thankfully now, in the LJS, a special service for children is held in tandem in a smaller sanctuary.

In Frankfurt's liberal synagogue women used to sit on the left side, men on the right. In orthodox temples women have to look down from a balcony upstairs. Those in the front row have to crane their necks for hours.

* * *

This was in the 20th century. My father, not a strong man, would remain in the synagogue all day; he had eaten his last meal before sun-set the previous day. He listened to the rabbi, clad in a white *kittle*, the garment worn on that Holy Day. Some male congregants wore prayer shawls round their shoulders, occasionally wrapping them round their faces while whispering Hebrew passages by heart. All men had their heads covered with either scull-caps or black hats. To a young child it seemed very mysterious, an experience which did not fit into the daily routine.

Before noon my mother took me home. I savoured the fresh air. My older brother after his *Bar Mitzwah* (confirmation at thirteen years of age) had to stay by my father's side. He never demurred, patiently waiting for the service to end.

In those days teenagers were not as sophisticated as the present generation. They did not have the advantage of downloading information. Knowledge was acquired with the help of books. They had to rely on their teachers and parents. The less gifted pupils were left behind; there was no provision for them in State schools. Wealthy parents employed tutors or students who were short of funds.

* * *

The serene, yet harmonious, atmosphere of the household was disrupted after the arrival of my mother's younger brother. Max, suitably named after one of the youngsters who played tricks on their unsuspecting victims in the German children's book '*Max und Moritz*', was high-spirited. He was the exact opposite of Richard, my father.

The Yom Kippur he was with us, while my parents were steeped in prayers, he chose to take us to *Café Laumer*. Instead of discreetly sitting inside, he chose a table on the terrace. His amusing tales made us laugh, in full view of passers-by on route to the synagogue, as well as shocked Christian Frankfurters. On that Holy Day I failed to understand what so thoroughly had upset my father. It was only when I was older that what Max believed to be a bit of fun was a complete disrespect for Jewish traditions.

* * *

Before I left my parental home in the summer of 1938 an incident occurred which is unforgettable. It certainly would not happen in the British Jewish community.

My father's business had folded mainly due to the boycott of Jewish enterprises. It is fair to mention that he had no business acumen; he would have been bankrupt sooner or later.

My parents were almost penniless and could not afford the Synagogue's yearly subscription. On my very last Yom Kippur with them in 1937 the whole family was refused admission to the service. After over eight decades I am still repulsed by the accountant's lack of understanding that some members of the congregation - and there must have been many - had their income and life-style reduced after the Nazis were in power.

* * *

In Paris I went to a synagogue only once. It may have been on Yom

Kippur. The memory is too vague to describe the service.

In 1939, all of us refugee children from a hostel in London had been evacuated. It was the beginning of WWII. The Holy Day passed by, unobserved by me, and this continued until I had married in March 1952. I became a member of the Liberal Synagogue off West End Lane. No subscription was demanded of me.

My cousin, a half-Jew - his mother was a Christian - fell in love with an Austrian Jewish refugee girl. She insisted that their son should be brought up as a Jew.

He and my daughter were about five years old when the four of us attended the Yom Kippur service. She stayed in the synagogue the whole day. I took the children home before lunch. My daughter, always obedient, held my hand as we progressed through the busy street. Not so her cousin: he balanced on the curb with one foot hobbling along near the traffic. He completely ignored my warnings and reprimand.

I did not bother to complain about his foolish behaviour to his mother; he would have denied it vehemently. His mother, as so often before, would have believed him, put him on her knees and consoled him, because he had been misunderstood by his stupid aunt.

* * *

Regularly my late husband and I attended the Yom Kippur service until both of us decided it had become too strenuous an effort for us. He fasted much longer than I did, until he realized it undermined his declining strength.

On my own over six years I carry on at an increasingly slower pace my daily tasks. This would be frowned upon by many of my fellow-Jews who fail to appreciate that the daily rhythm should not be interrupted even on THAT day. But I do mark the Holy Day by slowly walking through the neighbourhood, like I did so often with him during his life-time. The memories of Yom Kippurs past, since my childhood, flood into my mind.

Although it is now possible to assist the synagogue service on line, to me it is more meaningful to respect Yom Kippur in my very own way.

The Apple Tree

Every time I looked out of the bedroom window in October, my eyes feasted on the apple tree. This year the branches were weighted down by the bi-annual glut of small red fruit. I am not the only one to 'feast' at the sight. Sparrows descend on it regularly and take a bite out of one apple, fly away in order to attack another one.

This used to annoy my late husband. "They are destroying this year's harvest."

First he would knock at the window making a threatening noise. The birds did not even hear him through the double-glazed glass. His face became flushed with rage and he ran out. They flew away.

"Well, that's that! The pests have disappeared."

He was triumphant. As soon as he was indoors, they all returned.

* * *

During the first twenty-six years of our married life we occupied the top-floor of my mother-in-law's three-storey property. The front-door with a bell sealed us off from the nosiness of the elderly guests in her boarding house. She was very upset that easy access to her son was denied her.

At the back of the house was a garden. She and the old ladies - only once or twice had she been willing to offer a home to men - used to sit on a bench admiring the tulips and roses planted by a gardener. She was annoyed that with an able-bodied son she had to employ someone. Regularly they had rows.

"Why don't you take any interest in our garden. It upsets me to have to pay someone. After all, the rent I charge you is well below what your flat", and she stressed 'your flat' in a sarcastic voice, "is worth."

George used to shrug his shoulders and walk away.

"I have not finished with you yet," she used to shriek after him.

* * *

When we had moved into our own home he decided, "Now in my own property I take charge of the garden. But first we will have this wilderness cleared professionally."

Together we bought all the necessary gardening tools, chose plants and flower seeds. "Look, there is a little apple tree in bloom." He was very excited. "We must have our own apples. We'll buy that too."

Every day he was busy in the garden. A friend helped him to plant the tree in the most favourable spot. When he saw the first tiny apples on the branches he was overcome with joy. During his life he tended the garden like a mother does her new-born baby.

After he had passed away two lady-gardeners keep the flower beds free of weeds and tie the hanging branches of the growing apple tree.

One night in my dream the security light started to flash. I jumped out of bed and spotted from the window upstairs two suspicious characters peering through the gap in my fence. Their eyes were directed towards my apple tree. They appeared to be youngsters who might have wanted to steal the apples and sell them for a bit of pocket-money. They removed a panel of the wooden fence, ignoring the security light. Within a few minutes they pulled out the whole tree, ran with it through the gap and carefully replaced the panel with their gloved hands. No one could have caught them in time.

I woke up. "It's only a dream," I murmured. "The apples hang down like little red balls on a Christmas tree. All is safe."

The old Lady next door

Miss Jones, the old lady next door, always wore dark clothes under a striped navy pinafore. Blue eyes in her small, pale face looked down on our garden from an upstairs window every morning. As soon as we were outside, she used to trip towards us in her slippers through the back-room door. For a while she stood near her fence.

"We are your new neighbours, Helga and George. Just call us by our fist names."

"I am Miss Jones. Pleased to make your acquaintance," was her prim reply.

"She doesn't want to be too familiar. We must treat her with care," I suggested.

Invariably she appeared when one of us was outside to plant the vegetable seeds in the far corner. She seemed more knowledgeable than us amateur gardeners. We caught her as shook her head, but she refrained from giving us the benefit of her advice.

* * *

The first Sunday morning after we had moved in she informed us, "Sunday evenings our quartet assembles in my sitting room. We were professional musicians; now we often play at charity functions. We start about seven and finish around 10 o'clock. I hope it won't be a nuisance to you."

We assured her that we did not mind at all. In fact, I enjoyed listening to the classical chamber music which penetrated through the dividing wall.

A few months later it was our turn to apologize. We had double-glazing installed in all our rooms. However, the glass panes of our patio sliding door had been so badly fitted that we insisted they should be replaced.

"We are fully booked, sir. You will have to wait up to six weeks," the person at the other end of the line informed us.

"No way!" my husband shouted. "We are elderly people. There is a constant draft of cold air through the gap."

He threatened to take legal action.

"Alright! I will have to pay the lads over-time. Someone will take the exact measurements today and the new glass will be installed tomorrow after 6 p. m. We take great pride in always satisfying our customers."

* * *

Two men arrived in a large van shortly after the appointed hour. They removed the two panels without difficulty. As soon as they put the replacements into the metal frames, it was obvious that these, too, were not wide enough.

George went beligerent when they told us there is nothing more they could do that day.

"You intend to leave us unprotected? Anyone can take the panels out and enter this room." And again he threatened legal action. "I will also submit the matter to the Ombudsman for Fair Trading."

By that time it was nearly eight o'clock. They phoned their manager who had gone home. We heard them arguing with him. He had refused to go back to the warehouse so that they could load two larger panes to the sides of their van. Then they handed the phone to my increasingly irate husband. "You better have a word with him."

His renewed threats caused him to change his mind. He told the two men to return to the warehouse and take exact measurements under his supervision.

Half-an-hour later they came back with flood lights to enable them to work in the dark. The neighbourhood had been completely silent; the noise they made reverberated right round the area. At last they finished by eleven o'clock; peace rained again in the dimmed light of the street lamps.

Early in the morning George bought a big box of chocolate for Miss Jones. He rang her bell. He handed her the chocolates, apologizing profusely for the mayhem during the night. We were relieved that she accepted them, without saying a word.

* * *

In August we went on holidays to Switzerland for two weeks. On the last day we bought souvenirs for our friends and a beautifully carved little chalet for Miss Jones.

On our return, even before we unpacked our luggage, we knocked at her door.

"That's strange," I said when she did not open it. "She is nearly always at home. We'll try again later."

There was no sign of her the next day either, but a 'For Sale' board had been put into the front garden.

"She has probably gone to a nursing home. I wonder how we can find out her new address."

"Let's try the estate agent."

We followed up George's sound suggestion.

The estate agent told us that a gentleman had instructed his firm to put the house on the market. We asked for his client's telephone number.

"I am not authorised to give you his telephone number. But I will ring him, tell him that you are the deceased's neighbours and he might get in touch with you."

That same evening Mr. Jones, her nephew, contacted us.

"I do not live far away. May I come round to meet you?"

Within the next few minutes a very charming, middle-aged man arrived.

"It was a sad end for my aunt. She was all on her own when she fell. According to the doctor she must have been lying at the bottom of the stairs for at least a couple of days. I used to visit her after work twice a week. The agony poor aunt must have gone through! She was trying to pull herself towards the telephone in the hall with outstretched arms, but was too weak to reach it."

"If we had not been away we would have heard her shouting for help, or noticed that she did not come out into the garden." And we told him how she gradually became less reserved. After a short pause George added, "She never told us how we could contact her next of kin. All we could have done was to alert the police."

* * *

Like Miss Jones I did not want to leave my home nearly seven years ago after my husband passed away. She had been in the house all her life: with her parents and then with her widowed mother. She refused to go into a nursing or care home.

"She was independent; she lived for her music. Strangers she was wary of. There was no one locally to whom she entrusted her keys," said her nephew.

As soon as I was on my own I was given a pendant with a red button. It is connected to a Helpline which I can access through a box with a red light. Once a month I have to press the button to test it is in working order. Some forty years ago this may not have existed. Even if it did, she might have been afraid of 'prying eyes'.

In addition I had keys cut for friends and neighbours. They check up on me regularly. But, according to Mr.

Jones, his aunt had made no friends, except the three musicians.

"She did not even consider them as friends. To her they were colleagues, no more. I doubt whether there was any familiarity between them."

Did she feel safe, like I do? I hope she did in her reticent, peculiar way.

Jealousy

"I'm moving in with Alex," Jessica shouted upstairs.

Her parents were dressing their paraplegic son. Carefully they placed him on the stair-lift; fastening the safety-belt he was ready to be sent downstairs.Once landed, they would transfer him to another and push him into the lounge.

"I'm moving in with Alex - NOW," Jessica screamed again at the top of her voice, loud enough to wake the dead.

Gerry and Alice stopped in their tracks. Jessica stood by the open entrance door, a suitcase at her side. They hurried down. This had not been an idle threat like on previous occasions. Alice tried to put an arm round her pretty, eighteen-year old daughter's shoulders. Jessica shrugged it off.

"I'm leaving for good. You don't love me. You have no time for me.

It's always Eric this, Eric that. Alex loves me and I am in love with him."

"You are quite wrong, my darling. You are as precious to us as your brother. But he, poor lad, needs help round the clock. He is not able-bodied like you."

Her mother's soothing words were in vain.

"And I forbid you to live with a man who is nearly old enough to be your father. A sugar-daddy that's what he is. Do you want to be his kept woman", Gerry grinned.

"No, I'm not going to be a 'kept woman'," Jessica hissed full of venom. "The manager of the supermarket has offered me a permanent job as a cashier, once I have been trained."

Her parents were beside themselves. "And what about the place you have been offered at Bristol to study English Literature? Since your early childhood you had your nose in a book," her mother reminded her. And in a softer tone, "Please, darling, don't desert us."

"By the way, I not only hate the three of you; I hate the name you gave me. I am not a Shakespearian character."

Out she went. However, she did not tell her parents about the safety-net: she had not turned down her place at university, just in case.

For a few moments her parents remained helplessly by the closed door. They had been warned by the headmistress of Eric's school that such a scenario is not unusual.

"The siblings of so many handicapped students feel that they are being neglected. There are families where they refuse to communicate with their parents or are very disobedient. I know one case where a sister could not be left alone with her disabled brother because she might harm him. But in my twenty-year long headship no daughter or son has left home.

"I can only imagine how difficult it must be for you to be there for the fit daughter and at the same time give care to the disabled son." She looked at them with sincere compassion. "At least you have got her boy-friend's address."

"No, we haven't. We cannot even contact her. All we can hope for is that she will 'simmer down' and eventually get in touch with us. I cannot describe how upset we are and how often we ask ourselves what went wrong."

* * *

Eric was always eager to go to school. His hands were immobile. With great patience Mrs. Summers, the teacher, instructed him to use a computer with an eye-tracking screen. (The invalid's gaze controls the cursor to find letters, images or numbers on a lit grid.)

She watched him as he slowly did his work, constantly amazed at his thirst for knowledge in spite of his severe handicap. It encouraged her to tell his parents that he could also be coached at home and perhaps in the future he could even get a degree.

Money was no object. All the right equipment was bought; one of the younger teachers at the school taught him at home. Their son's commitment paid off: Eric was awarded a B.Sc. when he was twenty-six years old.

* * *

Alex, of medium height and broad-shouldered, with brown hair and sharp blue eyes in his pleasant, round face, regularly did his shopping in the nearby supermarket after work. To avoid the rush hour, he was in his office at eight o'clock and left about four in the afternoon, often taking files home. He was the head accountant in the London branch of a big international enterprise. His salary allowed him to live in a spacious maisonette in Kensington and enjoy a comfortable life.

Jessica had her tea-break at four o'clock. She never went into the staff canteen where the older women talked about their husbands and children. She had nothing in common with them. Although she was always smiling while dealing with shoppers, when alone she dreaded the moment she would arrive home to witness her parent's absorbing concentration on her brother's needs. Often tears would well in her eyes as she sat alone; or she would stare into the distance bemoaning her fate.

Alex had noticed the lonely girl with black hair and long lashes which shaded her dark eyes. One afternoon, while he pulled out a chair opposite her, he addressed her, "Are you crying?"

Jessica was moved that he, a complete stranger, seemed to take an interest in her, while at home she was freezed out. Over the following few weeks, she opened up to him.

"My parents don't love me. I am treated like a 'second fiddle'. They have only time for my brother. He is older than me and physically handicapped. As soon as I have earned enough money, I am going to find a place of my own."

"Well, I have a spare room; in fact several spare rooms. You can move into one of them whenever you like, and I certainly don't want your hard-earned cash."

It was like manna from heaven to be welcomed by this 'gorgeous' man with whom she had fallen in love. She was naive and unworldly, wrapped up in her own emotions.

Alex took her home with him. She was so grateful that after a week she insisted, "You do not need a cleaner to come twice a week. The least I can do is to do the household chores, some before and some after work."

Weekends they went shopping together. On fine days they drove out of London to walk in the nearby countryside and have lunch in a pub. The late teenager thought this was paradise and, although she had been a virgin, she did not reject his gentle advances and began to sleep with him.

Now, more relaxed, she chatted with one of her older colleagues in the staff canteen who had guessed that Jessica's circumstances had changed. She was a motherly type with a teenage daughter.

"I wish YOU were my mother, Mrs. Bolton. I certainly would have stayed at home."

"Call me Audrey. We don't need to be formal. Why did you leave home, dear?"

Jessica confided in her. "My parents don't care for me. That's why I moved in with Alex, my boy-friend," and she continued praising him and how happy she was.

Audrey listened to the young girls' flow of words. But when Jessica announced with pride that she alone was in charge of the household chores she felt it was necessary to curb the girl's enthusiasm. She abided her time, aware she had to find the right moment.

During a lunch-break Audrey observed, "Jessica you have lost a lot of weight. And you look a bit pale. Are you eating enough?"

"Of course, I am. Sometimes Alex prepares the meal; he is a better cook."

She anticipated the pleasure of sharing dinner with him without having to watch the unappetising manner in which Eric was being fed. "It used to put me off my food. My parents fussed over him with cajoling words. He had to be spoon-fed. I refused to do so."

* * *

Every Friday night Alex and his friends played poker. She did not like it when it was his turn to welcome them. They were loud and made a mess in the sitting room. Once she watched them, perched on her boy friend's knees. He kept on losing.

"Jessica, you bring me bad luck. You had better go upstairs." She slunk off unwillingly; it amused the other men. As she had forgotten to take up his mineral water, she came down again, eaves-dropping on their conversation.

"Alex, you lucky bastard," one of them cackled, "You've got a cleaner and bed-fellow - beg your pardon, a bed-lass - all in one. Tell me your secret. When are you proposing to the rich widow you have been stringing along for almost a year?"

Hilarious laughter sent her straight up the stairs; she pretended she had not heard them.

* * *

In the meantime an extension had been built at the rear of the house, as well as a shower-room with a hoist. Eric's aids had been installed in his new bedroom. His parents slept next door.

"What will become of him?" As they approached retirement age, it was a constant worry to them. "At the moment we are still strong enough to heave his unwieldy body about, but how much longer?"

Eric observed how they were ageing and began brooding about his future. He could not rely on his sister; her attitude towards him hurt him deeply. And that she had left home because of him made him very sad. He realized it was up to him to take the initiative.

"There are homes and flats adapted for people like me. Some of the older students live in them. Round the clock qualified carers look after the residents. It will be very hard for me to leave you, but I think the time has come when you ought to be relieved from the burden you carried since I was born."

That night they wondered why their daughter was so selfish, and their disabled son so thoughtful.

With Eric they viewed flats and care homes for severely disabled people. Many of them housed elderly people. These they judged to be most unsuitable. Finally they found what Eric felt was just right for him; nurses and carers were on call to assist the residents aged between twenty-one and thirty.

"Here I will feel comfortable. I would like to move in. It's lucky that one of the flats is empty."

He was thrilled that his future had been secured. "Of course, you can visit me. And, with me gone, Jessica might even decide to come back. On your way out look at the notice board! There are lectures, all sorts of entertainments. And, what is most important, I can bring all my IT equipment. I plan to research about my condition, even write about it, and..." he laughed, "yes, I have every intention to get it published in a medical journal with the title 'How to succeed in spite of a severe handicap'."

His cheerful tone was infectious. They did not argue with their son and put on brave faces. Their life which had revolved round him would be empty. How could they possibly fill the gap?

"We have to think hard what we will do with our lives. We must be positive:

Travel, when was our last holiday? Or perhaps, join a club or organisation?" They discussed their plans until late in the night.

* * *

Jessica tried to shut out the jibes, "You are a lucky bastard, to have a chivvy," and "When are you proposing to the rich widow you have been stringing along?" She was thunder-struck. His friend's banter wriggled round her brain-cells like worms. "So, I am here only on a temporary basis until he gets hitched to the widow. And what is in it for me?"

With a great effort of will she dried the tears which had welled out of her eyes. "You fool," she scolded herself. "I was such an easy prey for the man who befriended me in the cafeteria. I was seduced by his sympathy. But now, what is in it for me?" she repeated. "There is no bright future with him."

She was appalled by her own stupidity.

"This is a wake-up call! His pals have actually done me a favour."

Blinkers had fallen off her eyes. "And what do I do next?" she muttered.

Alex noticed a certain *froideur* in the girl's attitude; he could not pin-point why.

"You have become very quiet, no laughter. What's going on? Have you found a younger lover?" he joked as he opened his arms to embrace her. Even more bewildered when she did not react to his overture, again in a flippant voice, "Tell me what I have done wrong. I promise to mend my ways."

Silence.

"Ah well, if you behave like a stubborn, spoilt little child, I'll go to the pub. Come and join me when you

are your sweet, 'normal' self again."
He put on his jacket with a "Ta, ta, I
hope to see you soon."

Jessica was glad he had gone out. She
sat down and took stock of her
situation.

"I'm his play-thing. He's exploiting
me, my youthful ignorance. But, he
has really done me a favour: I have
grown-up; not anymore the silly girl
who exchanged her comfortable home
for this! What a fool I was!" She
could hardly believe that she had been
so gullible and naive. "But now to the
future!"

She planned that she would leave
him when he played poker in one of
his friends' house and return to her
family. "I realize they love me and
that my poor brother needs their
attention. How could I have been so
self-centred and blind? And I will try
my best to help him too."

The right moment came the following week when he would not be back until midnight. Jessica packed her bags and, like the 'Prodigal Son', returned home to a warm welcome. Her parents were overwhelmed with joy and thanked her over and over again for being with them again.

She was surprised how much had been changed to suit her brother's needs. All his aids had not yet been dismantled. Once more pangs of jealousy gripped her, however much her parents tried to make her feel as much loved as her sibling. But her resolve to be less jealous evaporated.

"Everything has been done behind my back. No one has consulted me," she shrieked.

"But, darling, you were not here. We didn't even know your address." She was too angry to listen to her mother who was trying to embrace her.

"I cannot remain here. It's my fault," she admitted. "I lack compassion."

Jessica was relieved that with foresight she had not refused the offer of a place to study.

"Anyhow, I am going to go Bristol and possibly take a gap-year. You'll be rid of me for at least three years," she threw in temper at her mother.

An audible sigh of relief accompanied her mother's response. "We will back you financially; just ask."

* * *

The idea of a gap-year did not appeal to her after all. All her energy was centred on trying to get on with her life and be independent. She immersed herself in 19th and 20th literature, was awarded a B. A. First Class Honours Degree and decided on post-graduate studies to enhance her job-opportunities. In her free time she worked in a cafeteria, relishing the camaraderie with the permanent staff.

When recruitment scouts from America interviewed her, they were impressed by her knowledge as well as her personality. She was offered a position at one of the most prestigious universities. It was, she felt, a god-sent chance to follow her destiny and get far away from her family who had neglected her and the oppressive atmosphere of sharing her life with her severely disabled brother.

Five years later she e-mailed her parents. "I am married and have a baby boy." She made no mention of Eric, nor did she indicate that they were welcome in her marital home.

"It's so sad," her mother lamented, "nothing would have prevented us from visiting her, now that Eric is settled in the care home."

"But at least," her husband consoled her, "Our daughter has found happiness after her tortuous past. She has realized her full potential and now lives, what we call, 'a normal' life, with her husband and baby."

In their mid-seventies they sold their house and decided to rent a sheltered flat where they could end their days. In spite of Jessica's lack of understanding, they believed they had acted wisely by giving their disabled son all the support he needed.

My Thanks to
Peter and Denise,
for their patience and advice.

Made in the USA
Columbia, SC
23 March 2018